## A SPOOKY SIGHT . . .

A cloud swept across the sky, obscuring the big, round orange moon. Suddenly there was only darkness. All motion among the horses stopped as abruptly as it had started. After a moment of stillness, there was movement in the center of the herd of wild horses, where a silvery stallion ran in circles and whinnied loudly. There was something about him, something odd. Lisa squinted.

"Did you see that?" She couldn't believe what her eyes were telling her, but there appeared to be a white-clad figure on the stallion's back.

"It was a rider," Kate said breathlessly, sitting forward in her saddle for a clearer view of the now almost invisible herd.

"Don't be silly—" Carole said, dismissing the claim.

"Pure silvery white, just like the horse," Lisa said. . . .

THE SADDLE CLUB

# GHOST RIDER

## BONNIE BRYANT

A BANTAM SKYLARK BOOK®
NEW YORK · TORONTO · LONDON · SYDNEY · AUCKLAND

*With special thanks for inspiration to the Usual Suspects:*
*Nicole and Marilyn*

RL 5, 009–012

GHOST RIDER
A Bantam Skylark Book / October 1992

Skylark Books is a registered trademark of Bantam Books,
a division of Bantam Doubleday Dell Publishing Group, Inc.
Registered in U.S. Patent and Trademark Office and elsewhere.

"The Saddle Club" is a trademark of Bonnie Bryant Hiller.
The Saddle Club design/logo, which consists of an inverted
U-shaped design, a riding crop, and a riding hat is a
trademark of Bantam Books.

ISBN 0-553-48067-7

Published simultaneously in the United States and Canada

Bantam Books are published by Bantam Books, a division of Bantam
Doubleday Dell Publishing Group, Inc. Its trademark, consisting of the
words "Bantam Books" and the portrayal of a rooster, is Registered in
U.S. Patent and Trademark Office and in other countries. Marca Regi-
strada. Bantam Books, 666 Fifth Avenue, New York, New York 10103.

PRINTED IN THE UNITED STATES OF AMERICA

OPM     0 9 8 7 6 5 4 3 2 1

## 1

MUSIC SWELLED TO *a crescendo, overwhelming the persistent flow of water. There was a flicker of light, barely perceptible through the cheap shower curtain. The bathroom door opened. And closed.*

*Swish! The shower curtain was thrust aside and in its stead appeared the long carving knife, which struck its target again and again. Dull, dark blood flowed mercilessly down the drain.*

"IT'S ONLY CHOCOLATE syrup, Dad!" Carole Hanson reminded her father as she sat down in the chair next to his.

"That may be, but it's *scary* chocolate syrup," Colonel Hanson said to her. He hefted a handful of popcorn from the bowl and munched happily, his eyes glued to the television.

Carole and her father were deeply involved in one of their favorite activities: watching an old movie together. This time, since it was almost Halloween, their choice was the Alfred Hitchcock classic thriller, *Psycho*. Carole had read all about how the "murder" in the old black-and-white movie had been staged by dripping chocolate syrup, instead of blood, into the shower. But, knowing that didn't take away from the tension, even for Carole, who closed her eyes. Her father was right: It *was* scary chocolate syrup.

The phone rang.

Carole was so startled by the interruption that she jumped. Then she laughed and so did her father.

"It's got to be a wrong number," he said. "Nobody who knows us would consider calling when *Psycho* is on television."

The ringing continued. "I'll get it," Carole volunteered. "I can't see this part anyway. My eyes are shut too tightly."

Colonel Hanson barely seemed to notice Carole's departure. She picked up the phone in the kitchen and said, "Hello."

"Carole, we need your help!" a familiar voice greeted her over the phone. It took Carole a few seconds to recognize the voice of her friend, Kate Devine. Kate and her family ran a dude ranch in the Southwest, two thousand miles from the suburb of Washington, D.C., where Carole and her father lived. It was hard to imagine what help Carole could be expected to give from such a distance.

"Sure," Carole agreed. "What can I do?"

"Well, it mostly has to do with my mother," Kate began. She was talking very fast because she was very excited. And because Carole was being flooded with information, it took her a few minutes to get the drift of it all, but when she did, she was so excited that *she* began speaking very fast, too.

"You mean you want us to come out there?" she asked. "To help your mother give a party? Of course, it's for a good cause. . . ."

It turned out that Kate's mother, Phyllis, had volunteered to be in charge of a Halloween Fair for all the children of Two Mile Creek—the town where The Bar None Dude Ranch was located—and the money the party made was going to be used to help create an after-school program for the Native American children who went to the local reservation school.

"There was a great activity center there," Kate explained, "but it burned down over the summer. The kids don't have any place to go. They've had to cancel the whole program. The trouble is that Mom doesn't know the first thing about running something like that. Then when I told her how The Saddle Club had helped Stevie run her school fair, well, she just about insisted. . . ."

Carole smiled, remembering. The Saddle Club was made up of Carole and her best friends—Stevie Lake and Lisa Atwood—but it also had some out-of-town members. Kate and her friend Christine Lonetree were two of them. The club had two requirements: The members had to be horse crazy, and they had to be willing to help one another whenever they needed it. Sometimes the help had to do with horses and horseback riding. Sometimes it had to do with schoolwork. Sometimes it even had to do with running school fairs. Now it appeared it was going to have to do with Halloween.

Stevie, Lisa, and Carole had visited the Devines' dude ranch several times. Kate's father, Frank, had been in the Marine Corps with Carole's father, and he was a pilot who occasionally flew a private plane. Whenever he came through Washington, he liked to combine the trip with a visit for his daughter and her friends. This time, Kate explained, her mom was planning to send him to pick up the girls.

"Wow. She *really* needs help, doesn't she?" Carole asked, now laughing at the thought that somebody as capable as Phyllis needed The Saddle Club to come to her aid. "You can count on us, you know."

"Oh, I know," Kate said. She paused, then added, "There's something else. . . . "

"What?" Carole asked, immediately feeling curious.

But Kate wasn't about to reveal anything. "I'll tell you about it when you get here," she replied.

Now Carole was even *more* curious, but she could tell that Kate was going to make her wait. She just had to find out what was going on, and that meant she was just going to have to convince her father, as well as Stevie's and Lisa's parents, to let them all go. They would have to miss three days of school; that would take some real convincing. Carole's mind raced. She'd found that spending time with Stevie meant she was learning to be a little bit devious, just as Stevie was. She had an idea.

"Hmm, school," Carole said. "I think your mother will be more convincing than I will be. Why don't we put her on the phone with my dad and let her do the work?"

"Great idea," Kate said. "I'll get her now."

"Hold it," said Carole. "On second thought, we'd better wait until *after* Dad finishes watching the movie that's on. I'll have him call back, okay?"

Kate understood. "I saw that *Psycho* is on television tonight. But it's not on until later here. If I'd known . . ."

Carole laughed. Her father was famous for his passion for old movies. "Don't worry. We'll call."

Carole finished her conversation with Kate and returned to the living room, where her father was gripping the arms of his chair as tightly as he had been when she'd left. She smiled to herself, even more certain that she'd done the right thing by not interrupting the movie. Idly Colonel Hanson passed the popcorn to his daughter, and they finished watching *Psycho* together.

As soon as it was over, however, she explained the situation.

"Three days of school?" her father said when she finished. "You'd need to miss three whole days?"

"But, Dad, it's for a good cause," Carole reminded him. She liked the sound of the phrase. It was true, and she felt it would be persuasive. "And remember, I have to do a certain number of hours of community service for school anyway. And, besides, one of those days is a teacher convention, so it's only two days that I would miss. Also, as you know, I've already finished my term project, due at the end of that week, and the class is bound to be spending a lot of time on that, so school would just be a waste of time for me anyway."

She paused to take a breath. "But if you are still worried about my missing the days, remember that we're studying immigration in the U.S. this year and the effect it's had on the land. You can't deny that what's happened to the Native Americans is related to that, so I'll have the chance to study the whole time I'm at The Bar None."

Colonel Hanson started laughing. "Very good," he said. "And when did you complete your study of persuasive rhetoric?"

"Huh?"

"I mean, you're doing a good job of presenting a solid argument with interesting facts to support your position. I'm impressed."

"Da-ad . . ."

As far as Carole was concerned, her father was the most terrific man in the world. They had always been close but had become even more so since the death of Carole's mother a few years before. They often joked and teased one another, and though Carole usually enjoyed it, she didn't think it was funny when something as important as three days off from school and a trip to The Bar None were at stake.

"I'll talk with Phyllis," Colonel Hanson said, sensing that this was what Carole really needed him to do.

It was all she could ask.

A few hours later it was all set, and Carole could barely believe her good luck. Neither could Stevie and Lisa. Somehow Phyllis Devine's call for help from The Saddle Club had struck a chord in everyone's parents, and they all had agreed. Each parent insisted on clearing it with the schools, but the girls were confident that if they kept repeating the sentence, "It's for a good cause," the schools would see the wisdom of letting the girls go.

"Isn't it wonderful?" Stevie squeaked into the phone.

"Fabulous!" Lisa agreed.

"Exciting," Carole added.

Stevie's family had signed up for a special telephone service that would let somebody talk to two people at once. The girls all agreed that it seemed custom-designed for telephone meetings of The Saddle Club. Her parents were beginning to think that the service had been custom-designed to make their telephone bill go through the ceiling, but as long as Stevie pitched in to pay for the phone bill, they didn't seem to mind.

"I've got zillions of ideas for a great Halloween party," Stevie said. "I mean, of course, we'll have a horror house, and then there should be a contest of some kind—like how about one where you guess the number of candy corns in a jar—and then there can be a pumpkin-carving table. . . ."

"Can we have kids decorate cupcakes?" Lisa asked. She was quite artistic and always enjoyed making things.

"And we should definitely offer pony rides," Carole said. Although all three of the girls were horse crazy, Carole was the horse craziest. She had a way of bringing horses into everything she did. Her friends liked that about her.

"There should be a costume contest, too," Lisa said. "And a parade."

"Definitely a parade," Stevie agreed. "And we can lead it."

"What should we wear?" Lisa asked.

"You sound like Veronica diAngelo," Stevie said. "That's all she ever thinks about. Are you catching it from her?" Veronica was a snobbish rich girl who also rode at Pine Hollow. She was always more concerned about how she looked than how she rode. That was definitely *not* how Stevie, Lisa, and Carole thought about riding.

"I don't mean that we should go out West dressed as fashion plates," Lisa said. "I mean that if it's a Halloween party, we're going to need costumes. Frankly, I'm tired of being a ballerina every Halloween."

"Is that what you were?" Stevie said. "You're so lucky! The only costumes we ever have around this place are leftover pirate outfits from my brothers."

"And it seems like I'm always going as a noncommissioned officer," Carole lamented. Colonel Hanson seemed to have unlimited access to leftover Marine Corps uniforms.

"Come on, girls, we can do better than *this*," Lisa said.

"Hmmmm," Stevie said. It was a sign that her scheming mind was working. "Why don't we use Veronica as an inspiration?"

"Ugh," Carole said.

"And go as models? Dressed in designer clothes our parents can't afford?"

"No, that's not what I mean at all," said Stevie. "You know how Veronica is always accusing us of being goody-goodies for Max?" Max was the owner of Pine Hollow. Stevie, Lisa, and Carole always wanted to please him because that meant they were learning more about horses, but only Veronica would have called them goody-goodies. "You know how she even calls us the three blind mice?"

There was a brief silence while Lisa and Carole figured out what was on Stevie's mind.

"Great idea!" Lisa said. "All we'll need are some gray sweats."

"Hooded shirts that we can put ears on . . . ," Carole suggested.

"Whiskers!" Stevie added.

"Add sunglasses, a cane, and, *voilà*! There you have three blind mice."

"Stevie, you're brilliant," Lisa said.

"It was nothing," Stevie said. "Just the logical thing to do. Well, just the logical thing for a *genius* to do. . . ."

"And so modest," Lisa teased.

"I have to be careful, though," Stevie said. "I can't use up all of my genius tonight."

"Are you afraid you're about to run out?" Lisa asked.

"Not really. It's just that I'm going to need inspiration. See, my parents said *I* have to be the one to talk Miss Fenton into letting me out of school for three days next week."

Lisa and Carole laughed. If there was ever anybody who was an expert at talking a grown-up into letting her do something the grown-up really didn't think she ought to do, it was Stevie.

"I don't think there's any danger of your running out of genius for *that*," Carole said.

"Just tell her it's for a good cause," Lisa suggested.

". . . AND, MISS FENTON, it's for a good cause," Stevie found herself saying the next morning. She was standing in Miss Fenton's office, trying to sound sincere. She was sincere. She meant everything she had said, even the part about making up missed work before returning to school on Monday. She just wanted to be sure she sounded as sincere as she felt.

Miss Fenton cleared her throat. Stevie didn't think that was a good sign. "All right, now, Stephanie, let me see if I've got this straight."

The fact that Miss Fenton was calling her by her full name also wasn't a good sign. Nobody *ever* called her Stephanie unless there was trouble.

"You are promising to do all the work you miss *and* an extra report about the value of community service, so that you and your friends can take three days off from school to travel two thousand miles to give a party?"

"And it's for a good cause," Stevie added again.

Miss Fenton sighed. That was definitely not a good sign. "Well, the only thing I can say is that, considering what you've done at Fenton Hall in the name of good causes, I hope these poor people know what they're in for!"

It took Stevie a second to realize that she'd actually been given permission to go. "Oh, they do, Miss Fenton, they do!"

Then Miss Fenton laughed and shook Stevie's hand. "Good luck, Stevie," she said. "It sounds to me as if you've got an opportunity to make a special contribution to a worthy cause. I wouldn't think of standing in your way, and I can't wait to read your report. Next Monday morning."

The significance of the last sentence was not lost on Stevie. She smiled, nodded, and dashed out of Miss Fenton's office. She didn't want to wait around for Miss Fenton to have a change of heart!

WHENEVER THE GIRLS arrived at The Bar None, they got a warm greeting, but this one was particularly warm. The look on Phyllis Devine's face when The Saddle Club came into view was total relief.

"I thought you'd never get here!" she exclaimed, hugging all three girls at once.

The girls laughed. "You can count on us," Stevie promised. "Anytime. I mean anytime it's going to get me out of school for three days! Now here's what I've got planned."

Ideas poured out of Stevie the way water flowed over Niagara Falls. The girls hadn't even put their suitcases down before Stevie got to the horror house, which was going to be completely dark and *very* scary.

". . . and for that, we're going to have to peel some grapes—eyeballs, you know. Cold pasta makes great 'brains' in the dark, but I think we ought to use something other than spaghetti. What's that stuff that looks like brains? Radiatore or something? We'll have the kids screaming from here to Denver!"

"But won't they be scared?" Phyllis asked.

"That's the whole idea," Stevie assured her. "Of course, we'll make sure that it's all fun and they know it. We can't have everybody fainting all day long. Now about the crafts tables . . ."

Stevie and Phyllis sat down at the kitchen table and began plotting. As Stevie rattled off her ideas, Phyllis nodded enthusiastically and took notes.

"Where do these go?" *Thump.* The girls heard the sound of their suitcases hitting the floor and looked to see who had asked the question. It was a boy a little older than they were.

"This is John Brightstar," Kate said, introducing him to Stevie, Lisa, and Carole. "His father, Walter, is our new head wrangler." She thanked John for bringing the bags in and told him that the girls were staying in Bunkhouse One. Lisa offered to give him a hand carrying the suitcases over to the bunkhouse. John accepted her offer. Without a word the two of them picked up the suitcases and left the kitchen.

". . . and we're going to need to have at least one

really special prize. It's for the Kandy Korn Kounting Kontest," Stevie continued, as she and Phyllis picked up exactly where they'd left off.

Carole turned to Kate. "Okay, what's up?" she asked. "I mean, it's time for you to explain what you meant by 'There's something else.'"

Kate's face lit up. "It's really exciting," she said. "It's about a horse. Come on, I'll tell you all about him."

The look on Kate's face told Carole that this was a very special horse, and she couldn't wait to hear more. The two of them left the party schemers at the kitchen table and retreated to the lounge, where they could talk about something *really* important: horses.

"It's a stallion," Kate began. "He's pure white, and he's the most beautiful horse I've ever seen."

"Really white?" Carole asked. The only true white horses were albinos and were extremely rare. All the rest were called gray horses, no matter how white they appeared, because they all had some other colors mixed in with the white.

"A really white gray," Kate confirmed. "But it isn't even so much his color as his beauty."

Carole could visualize the horse, and she was thrilled for her friend. "When did you get him?" she asked.

"I didn't. That's the problem," Kate said. "He's in a

wild herd that roams on the federal land around here. I *want* to get him. I just don't know if I can."

"Isn't there a way to buy a wild horse?" Carole asked. "I remember reading something about it."

Kate nodded. "You don't buy them. You *adopt* them. It's a program run by the Bureau of Land Management." She pulled a booklet out of a pile on a coffee table. It was entitled *So You'd Like to Adopt a Wild Horse or Burro.* Carole flipped through it, and it sparked her memory. She had read about the Adopt-a-Horse-or-Burro program. If somebody wanted a horse, all he or she had to do was pay a small adoption fee and take good care of the horse for a year, at which time that person could own it. There were other rules, but it wasn't much more complicated than that. The only drawbacks were that the horses were most likely completely wild, and you might not get too much choice.

"The next adoption is coming up in another week, and I just keep thinking, what if somebody else adopts him before I do?" Kate said.

Carole looked at her friend and smiled. "This is almost funny, you know," she said. "You've been a national championship rider. You've been mounted on some of the finest horses in the country with bloodlines that would wow the queen of England. And now you've got your heart set on a no-account mustang?"

Kate nodded. "He's special," she said.

"Love at first sight?" Carole asked.

"Definitely," Kate said. "Just wait until you see him."

"How long do I have to wait? Can we go for a ride now?"

"I thought you'd never ask," Kate said. "Let's get Stevie and Lisa."

IT TOOK THE girls a very short time to change into their riding clothes and head for the barn to saddle up their horses. Each one had chosen a favorite horse on previous visits to The Bar None, so there was no delay in selecting their mounts for this ride. Kate had alerted Walter, and their horses were ready for them.

Carole greeted Berry, her strawberry roan, with a firm pat. Chocolate, Lisa's bay mare, nuzzled her neck.

"She remembers me!" Lisa cried, offering the horse a sugar lump.

"Possibly, but she may also be able to smell the sugar," Kate said wryly.

Lisa was just pleased to see "her" horse again.

Stevie rode a brown-and-white-patched pony whose name was Stewball. He had an offbeat look that matched his personality, which also matched Stevie's. This horse always seemed to know exactly what he wanted to do. Normally that was a troublesome characteristic in a horse. The odd part about Stewball was that what he wanted to do always seemed to be exactly what Stevie wanted to do. It was as if the two of them were made for each other. Back in Virginia, Stevie usually rode a blue-blooded Thoroughbred named Topside. Topside was an elegant, beautifully trained horse. He was almost the opposite of Stewball. Stevie loved them both for very different reasons. She gave Stewball a great big hug when she caught him in the paddock. He pretended not to notice, but Stevie was convinced he remembered her and was at least a little bit happy to see her again.

John was at the barn ready to help the girls saddle up their horses while his father rounded up Kate's horse from the field. When John offered to bring Lisa her saddle, she accepted. Western saddles were much heavier and more cumbersome than the English ones they used at Pine Hollow. Lisa was glad for the help— until John showed up carrying a pony saddle!

"Uh, John," Kate began.

It was then that Lisa noticed the twinkle in his eyes. "I just thought these fancy English rider types might prefer a little saddle to a real one," he said.

Stevie was the first one to laugh. She herself was quite a practical joker, and she always appreciated it when somebody thought up something funny to do.

"Thanks, but we can handle the real thing," Lisa

said. "And I guess I'm going to have to get it myself. . . ."

John smiled wryly. "No problem," he said. "I'll get it for you."

"John! What's going on?" Walter demanded, returning to the paddock with Kate's horse, an Appaloosa named Spot.

"We were just joking around, Walter," Kate said. "John's helping my friends saddle up."

"It doesn't look like he's being much help," Walter said. His sternness surprised Stevie, Lisa, and Carole. "It looks more like he's causing trouble."

"No trouble, Walter," Kate said. "It's just fun."

Walter grunted a response while he hitched Spot's lead rope to the corral fence. Then he fetched the Appaloosa's saddle and had him saddled up in what seemed like an instant.

"Wow," Carole said, admiring how quickly he'd done the job.

"Just trying to be helpful like I'm supposed to be," Walter said, holding Spot's reins so Kate could mount him.

John looked sheepishly at his father.

Kate climbed into the saddle and thanked Walter. It took only a few more minutes for Lisa, Stevie, and Carole to mount up, too. Then Walter and John helped them all adjust the cinches on the saddles, and they were off.

It was wonderful. Stevie, Lisa, and Carole loved riding in any form, and they particularly loved the kind of riding they did at Pine Hollow. But riding at The Bar None was unique. They weren't riding through fields and hilly woods. They were riding across Southwestern desert, passing tall cactus and scrubby bushes, around old rocky mountains, and along dusty trails. It was open, it was wild. Lisa found herself thinking that she had suddenly been dropped into an old Western movie. She could easily imagine cowboys and stagecoaches and one-street towns and half-expected John Wayne to pop up in front of her and drawl, "Howdy, pilgrim."

She smiled at her own thoughts and recognized that it felt great to be back at The Bar None, riding with Kate and her friends.

Kate's voice abruptly broke into Lisa's daydream. She was talking about the herd of wild horses and the one she wanted to adopt. Lisa listened with interest.

"The Bureau of Land Management has to keep down the wild-horse population," Kate was explaining. "If there are too many horses out there, two things will happen. First, the land won't support a large number, and some of them will die. Second, they'll eat everything that's growing, and the land will be even more barren. That's why the government likes to make the horses available to people who can give them good homes."

"It sounds like a great program," Carole said.

"It is," Kate confirmed. "Both the horses and the land benefit—to say nothing of us lucky ones who get the horses!"

"So when can we see your stallion?" Stevie asked.

"The herd has been collecting by the rise across the creek every afternoon recently," Kate replied. "We should find them there about now."

"Just show us the way," Stevie said. Then an odd look crossed her face. "On second thought, I don't think you have to. I have the feeling that Stewball knows exactly where to find them. He's in gear."

That was just like Stewball. Once he had an idea in his head, he was as stubborn as Stevie—and as likely to be right about it, too. All the riders decided to let Stewball take the lead. They trotted along a trail that followed a two-lane highway for a good distance, and then Stewball took a right and aimed for a mountain. He certainly seemed to know what he was doing, and when he rounded the base of the mountain and entered a small green valley where Two Mile Creek ran, they found that he was absolutely right. There, drinking lazily from the sparse stream, was a herd of about fifty wild horses. The girls drew their horses to a halt and watched.

It took Lisa's breath away. She knew about natural herds. She'd read about them. She'd even seen an educational special on them. But she'd never seen one. She'd seen hundreds, even thousands of horses in her life, but she'd never seen one that didn't belong to someone, hadn't been trained, coddled, shod, cared for. And here were fifty horses who didn't belong to anybody. There were no halters, no shoes, no feed boxes, no vets, no riders. These animals were wild. They didn't live in paddocks and stalls. They didn't eat processed grains and sugar lumps. They lived here. They lived everywhere. Lisa was stunned by the sight, and she wasn't alone in her thoughts.

"Oh." Stevie sighed. "They're beautiful."

"Where's the gray?" Carole whispered.

"Watch," Kate said.

The wind shifted then and carried their scent. Some of the mares lifted their heads and sniffed. They whinnied gently. Then the horses began moving around. The mares drank again. And then a pure white head rose, sniffed, and looked. The horse's ears twitched like antennae, reaching to pick up any sound. The girls were silent, but the horse found them anyway. The stallion called to his brood. At the instant of his call, all the horses in the herd were alert, awaiting his signal. Then, rising as if by magic, the pure white horse jumped and neighed loudly. And then the whole herd began to move, galloping off and away from the riders by the mountainside. The only sound in the desert was the thunder of hoofbeats, and then all that remained was the cloud of dust they left behind.

"Oh," Lisa said breathlessly.

"Just what I was going to say," Stevie agreed.

3

"YOU'VE JUST GOT to have him," Lisa said to Kate as they rode back toward The Bar None. "He's so beautiful. . . ."

"Did you notice the nick in his ear?" Kate asked. "It's very distinctive. It's like the imperfection that makes him absolutely perfect."

At first Lisa didn't think that was a very logical description, but as she thought about the horse, she came to think that Kate was right. Part of what made the stallion so beautiful was the wildness, and certainly the scar was a symbol of that, and would always be, even after Kate owned him and trained him.

Then, as if Carole had heard Lisa's thoughts, she

asked Kate, "Will you train him yourself? Do you know how to do it?"

"I know some things, of course," Kate said. "I mean, you can't spend as much time around horses as I have, or even as you have, without knowing a lot about training."

"Training a wild horse has got to be different from training a domestic one," Stevie reasoned. "I mean, that stallion has never stood still for a human in his life. It's hard to imagine that he ever will, either."

A smile crossed Kate's face, which told her friends that Stevie had put her finger on something very important to Kate: the stallion's very wildness.

"He will," Kate said. "I know it. Besides, Walter said he'd help me. He's had lots of experience with wild ponies. He knows what he's doing."

The mention of Walter reminded the girls of the awkward confrontation between him and John at the stable earlier.

"Is he always that serious?" Stevie asked. "He came down pretty hard on John."

Kate nodded. "I think Walter feels he has to prove himself. See, he's got some kind of odd reputation."

"You mean like he's dangerous?" Lisa asked.

"No way," said Kate. "But there's definitely something mysterious about his past."

"How do you know?" Stevie asked.

"We don't. That's what's mysterious," Kate explained. "Neither Walter nor John will talk about it at all, but it has something to do with John's mother. She's dead, I think. I overheard some parents talking about it at school, but as soon as they saw me, they stopped talking."

"Too bad they saw you," Stevie said. One of Stevie's favorite activities was overhearing conversations not intended for her. She was disappointed that Kate had been discovered.

"It didn't make any difference," Kate said. "From what I heard, it was clear they didn't know anything anyway. It's all just gossip. My parents don't listen to gossip, so they hired Walter, and nobody's sorry they did. He's a hard worker, and John works even harder. Sometimes I feel sorry for them because they work so hard and nothing ever seems to get better. Walter is always grim and determined. John? Well, he's nice and helpful, but he's hard to get to know."

"He seems lonely," Lisa said.

Stevie nodded. "That must be why he tried that practical joke. He just wanted to be friendly."

"That's what I thought," Lisa said.

Carole wrinkled her nose. "Well, it wasn't very funny. The saddle you put on a horse is very important. It needs to fit the horse, and it needs to fit the rider. I don't think it's something to joke about. I mean, if the saddle doesn't fit a horse, the horse can get sores, and they take a long time to heal—"

"Carole!" Stevie said, a little exasperated. "It was a joke."

Carole loved horses so much that it was harder for her to understand joking about them than it was for her friends. It was just like her to go off on a long speech about horse care and lore. Her friends took it as their responsibility to bring her back to reality.

"Definitely a joke," Kate assured her.

"And a slightly funny one," Lisa agreed. "It made me laugh."

"Well, Walter didn't laugh," Carole said.

"But he's *always* serious," Kate said.

"I wonder what secret he and John are keeping," mused Stevie. Her friends looked at her. There was nothing Stevie loved more than a mystery she could solve. There was nothing she hated more than not having her curiosity satisfied.

"Stevie!" Lisa said. "Some things just aren't any of our business. I mean, you have to respect other people's privacy."

"I suppose," Stevie conceded. "I'll mind my own business. I promise."

"Well," Kate said, "our business right now is to finish this ride and get back to the ranch. Christine's coming over later tonight, and Mom said something about wanting some help in the kitchen for dinner. Any volunteers?"

Three hands went up. Helping Phyllis cook was always a pleasure because the results were always so mouth watering, and, as they thought about it, it had been a long day for the travelers. Some good food would be very welcome. They headed home.

"IT'S A HEART!" Stevie declared.

"No, an oval—I mean an egg! A penny, uh, a saddle!" Carole suggested.

"A heart with some lumps around the edge—five lumps around the edge?" Stevie persisted.

Lisa shook her head violently. She scribbled some more and then looked to Kate for help.

"A treasure map?"

The girls were playing Pictionary. They were one team. The other team had been made up from other guests at The Bar None. The other guests were definitely winning, and Lisa didn't think her friends would ever recognize the turtle she was trying to draw. She drew a pattern on the turtle's back that looked pretty realistic to her.

"A bathtub!" Stevie was triumphant. But wrong. Lisa shook her head.

Now desperate, she tried drawing a hare to suggest a tortoise. That was no more successful.

"Time!" the other team announced.

"A turtle," Lisa said. Her friends looked at her scribbly sketch with a new point of view. "Three years of art lessons and I can't draw a recognizable turtle."

"Don't feel bad," Stevie told her. "Remember, I had trouble drawing a bell. This game is not about great art."

"Yes it is," a member of the opposing team chimed in—and then smiled gleefully. Considering all the very odd scribbles that had passed for pictures since the game started right after supper, everybody knew that was funny, and they all laughed.

The person who was drawing for the other team reached for a card, frowned as she looked at it, and then asked Lisa to time the round. Lisa automatically looked at her wrist. There was nothing there. It didn't make any difference in the game since they were actually using an egg timer, but it did make a difference to her wrist. She'd obviously taken her watch off sometime, and she had to try to remember where and when.

She flipped the egg timer and set her mind to work while the other team struggled with a drawing of a vegetable peeler.

*Pencil. Sword. Lollipop. I mean sucker—you know, the kind with a looped handle. Pot. Pan. Knife.*

Lisa remembered that she'd had it on when she and

her friends had been riding. She didn't remember whether she'd had it on when she was working in the kitchen and at dinner.

*Lasso. Lasso roping an egg. Lasso laying an egg.*

She recalled unsaddling Chocolate and noticing how much lather the horse had worked up. She'd given her a bath, and that must have been when she removed her watch. The memory came back then. She had taken her watch off and hooked it on a nail protruding from a wall in the barn. She didn't remember taking it off the nail, so it was almost certainly still there. It would probably still be there in the morning, but Lisa didn't want to take the chance.

*Toothbrush. Knife. Kitchen something. It's a—it's a— cheese grater? Whisk? Spatula? Rolling pin. No, not that. I mean—peeler. It's a vegetable peeler!*

Lisa had to smile at the way the other team all gave one another high fives for coming up with vegetable peeler. The sketches were unrecognizable to her, but it was enough to make it clear that they had won the match. Kate, Lisa, Stevie, and Carole all conceded good-naturedly and then politely refused the opportunity to get whupped again.

"Tomorrow we'll try Monopoly," Stevie said. Then she turned to her friends and whispered loudly, "I'm a shoe-in to pick up Boardwalk and Park Place, and we won't have to draw a *thing!*"

"Now wait a minute. Do you play 'Free Parking'?" asked one of their potential opponents.

As the members of the two teams cheerfully battled over the rules for playing Monopoly, Lisa slipped out of the room. She wanted to get out to the stable to find her watch.

She picked up a flashlight in the kitchen, slipped into a stable jacket, and walked out into the dark, cold desert night. Lisa pulled the warm collar up around her neck and stuck her hands into the oversized jacket pockets. She didn't need the flashlight as long as she was outdoors. The sky was clear and completely studded with stars. The moon, nearly full, shone down on her, engulfing the whole ranch in its silvery beams. She could see her own breath turn to steam.

The barn was completely dark, and since Lisa had no idea where the light switches were, she clicked the button on the flashlight and looked around her, trying to accustom her eyes to the shadowy darkness. She knew the barn well in daylight. In the dark it was totally unfamiliar, almost threatening.

Just because it's almost Halloween doesn't mean there are ghosts in the barn, she told herself. She almost believed it, too. She shivered and tried to orient herself so she could recall exactly where the nail was that she had used to park her wristwatch.

The stomp of a horse's foot on the wooden floor

made her jump. But then there was a whinny, and the sound was so familiar that Lisa found it strangely comforting.

"There, girl, there," came a human voice.

That startled Lisa even more. She'd thought she was alone.

"Who's there?" the voice called out quietly.

"It's me," Lisa said, and then realized that that wasn't much of an identifier. "Lisa. Lisa Atwood. Who are you? Where are you?"

"It's John. And I'm with the mare over here."

Lisa turned to the sound of his voice. She blinked in the darkness and then noticed a warm glow coming from the box stall at the end of the barn. She found John there, sitting on a stool in the stall. A mare, almost ready to foal, stood nearby, shifting from one side to the other uneasily.

"She seemed restless," he said. "I don't think she's ready yet, but she calmed down when I came in. I figured she just wanted company." There was a small lantern at his feet.

He reached up and casually patted the mare on her forehead. She nodded slowly.

"Sometimes they get that way," John went on. "It can't be easy having a great big foal in her womb, almost ready to be born, but not quite. Mothers have it tough, you know."

Lisa knew. She'd helped at the birth of a foal once. It had been one of the most exciting experiences of her life, and all during it she'd felt the anxiety and discomfort of the mare, who still seemed to bear it all willingly because there was no other choice. Lisa was also struck by the way John had expressed his concern—*mothers* have it tough. It made her recall Kate's suspicion that the rumors about John's father had to do with his mother. It wasn't any of her business. She pushed the thought back.

"Should your father know about this?" Lisa asked.

"Nah. He's sleeping. I'll take care of the mare tonight. He needs the rest. She needs the care." He patted the mare again. Then he looked quizzically at Lisa. "What are you doing here? Shouldn't you be getting into some hot game of charades or something?"

"Pictionary," she said. "We lost. I think I left my watch out here this afternoon. I put it on a nail somewhere, and I can't remember exactly where."

"Gold watch. White face. Black leather band?"

"Yes."

"Haven't seen it."

Lisa couldn't help herself. She laughed. John had a dry sense of humor that tickled her.

Slowly he stretched out his right leg and reached into the pocket. "Here it is," he said, handing her the watch. "I figured it was yours, and I figured you'd be back out here in the morning. I didn't want to leave it hanging there by the hose all night long. Never can tell who might sneak in here just to see what the dudes have left hanging around. . . ."

"Thanks," Lisa said, slipping the watch back onto her wrist and buckling it. John stood up then and stepped out of the box stall. He closed the door softly behind him so as not to disturb the mare, who was now sleeping soundly. He stood near Lisa, and she found herself very aware of him. He was tall with sharp dark features. A shock of black hair hung straight over his eyes. His eyes seemed to see everything, and his gentle smile reassured Lisa. She felt as if she were the mare, being put at ease by this very interesting young man.

"It's a little spooky out here in the dark," Lisa said.

"Don't worry," John teased her. "I'll fend off any bats or gremlins who try to attack you or drink your blood."

"What a relief you're here," she teased him back.

"I'll also walk you back to the main house," John offered. Lisa was surprised to find that that was just what she'd been hoping he'd say.

"Did you girls have a nice ride this afternoon?" John asked as they headed back outside.

"Oh, yes," Lisa told him. "We went out and found the herd of wild horses—the ones that are going to be put up for adoption. You know about that?"

John nodded.

"Well, Kate has her heart set on the stallion. What a beauty he is—pure white, with this wonderful nick in his ear."

"No," John said abruptly.

"Sure, it's his right ear."

"No," he repeated. "She can't."

Lisa was startled by the sharpness of his voice. The gentle young man who was tending to the mare and escorting Lisa back to the house had suddenly disappeared. Lisa could feel his tenseness—almost anger. He halted and faced Lisa squarely. For a second she was almost afraid of him.

"What's the matter?" she asked.

"The stallion. She can't have him. You can't let her do it."

"Why not? What is going on here?" Then Lisa thought she knew what was going on. "Now, look. If you want that stallion, you've got every right, just the same as Kate, to try to adopt him yourself. All you have to do is register. I'm sure your father would do it for you because you have to be eighteen, but it doesn't cost much, and—"

"I don't want the stallion," John said. "And Kate can't have him, either. Don't you see?"

"No, I don't," Lisa said. "That's a beautiful horse. I

watched him protecting his mares, and I watched him gallop. He's going to make a fabulous saddle horse. Kate's going to love owning him, and imagine what it's been like for him to live in the wild—"

"It's where he belongs," John said. "It's where he's got to stay."

In her mind Lisa replayed the scene they'd come upon this afternoon: the stallion in the middle of his brood, king of all he surveyed, master of the mountains, ruler of the plains, untamed, unowned. Then she remembered what Kate had said about the very real possibility of the horses dying on their own.

"I know why they put horses up for adoption," John said, as if he were reading her mind. "It's a great program and it's well done. The problem isn't the program, it's the stallion with the nick in his ear. Kate can't have him. Nobody can. Just his rider . . ."

"I don't understand," Lisa said.

"Of course you don't. But don't let her do it."

"What—"

John spun on his heel and was gone, walking off in the darkness, returning to the barn, to the mare, to his own secret thoughts. Lisa was about as confused as she'd ever been. Who was this boy who felt the unease of a mare about to foal, kidded about saddles, picked up watches for safekeeping, walked young girls to safety in the dark, and had a mysterious notion about a stallion with a nick in his ear? What did it all mean?

A cold wind whipped through the moonlight and chilled Lisa to the bone. It was time to go back to the main house, alone.

LATER THAT NIGHT Christine Lonetree joined the girls in their bunkhouse for a Saddle Club meeting. This one looked more like a pajama party than a meeting, because that's exactly what it was.

All five of them were in warm nightclothes—mostly sweatpants and sweatshirts. It was October, and Bunkhouse One was heated only by a small potbellied stove and a fireplace. That didn't matter to the girls, though. They were too busy discussing plans to pay much attention to the occasional chatter · of teeth. They also knew that the minute they climbed into their down sleeping bags, they'd be toasty warm. They just weren't ready to go to sleep yet. There were too many things to talk about.

"It's this incredible sort of dollhouse that my mother made," Christine said. She was trying to describe her mother's latest project. Mrs. Lonetree, in addition to teaching modern European and Russian history at the regional high school, was a potter. Sometimes she made what tourists thought were traditional Native American crafts. Most of the time, though, she did more original and creative work. She also worked with the children at the reservation's after-school program, when there was a program. Now Christine was telling them about an adobe dollhouse that Mrs. Lonetree had crafted.

"It's got two levels. Both of them are open so you can see what's inside, and it's a good thing, too, because she's completely filled it with traditional decorations. I mean blankets, wall hangings, even miniatures of the pots she sells to the tourists. It's incredible, and it's for you—for your party, I mean."

"It's going to be the big prize," Stevie said. "Kids will be lining up clear to the state line just to guess the number of candy corns in the jar. It's going to make zillions of dollars for the after-school program. Your mother is amazing—and wonderful. I can't wait to see it." Stevie reached for the bag of marshmallows, speared two with the long-handled fork, aimed the fork at the fire's embers, and carefully began turning them a perfect golden brown while the girls continued to chat about the Halloween Fair.

Once they had decided on several more activities—an archery game with pumpkins for targets, costume parade, and a makeup table—their thoughts naturally turned to the scarier aspects of the season. They turned off all the lights, lit a candle, and began to tell ghost stories.

Stevie was the hands-down winner in any ghost-story-telling competition. When her turn came, her four friends listened in total attention throughout. Finally she came to the conclusion of her story and lowered her voice to an almost inaudible hush. Lisa leaned forward, straining to catch every spellbinding word.

". . . and then a second rush of cold air swept through the castle and carried off Count Boscovich, Dante, and the raven. Miranda was alone in the castle, and all that remained to remind her of the horror she'd witnessed was the scratch on her face. And to this day, every time there is a full moon on Halloween, three drops of blood flow from Miranda's cheek. One is for her lover, one is for her father, and one is for the raven. It is the only proof she has that any one of them ever lived."

Suddenly a gust of cold air rushed through the cabin,

blowing out the candle. Lisa screamed. A second later footsteps approached and the bunkhouse door flew open. This time Lisa and Carole both screamed.

"Are you okay?" someone asked.

The ceiling light flipped on. It took a few seconds for the girls' eyes to adjust to the light, but when they could see again, they found that John Brightstar was standing there, and he looked very concerned. In fact he looked so solemn that it was all the girls could do to keep from giggling. Stevie actually couldn't restrain herself. Kate and Carole joined in.

Lisa could feel a blush of embarrassment rise on her cheeks. "We're fine," she began. "We were telling ghost stories," Stevie's very good at it, and she managed to scare me. Then when the candle went out, well, it just startled me." Suddenly it struck Lisa that it was very odd that John should just show up. Had he been passing by and heard her scream? She wanted to ask him what he was doing there, but he spoke again before she had the chance.

"You were telling ghost stories?" he said eagerly. "Great. I have a story I want to tell you." With that, he sat down on the floor, joining the circle the girls had formed around the fire. He cleared his throat and began.

Many years ago, so many my grandfather does not remember it, there were two tribes who lived and battled one another in these lands. They had warred for so long that nobody could remember when they had not warred. Neither could anyone remember why they warred. So deep were their hatred and fear that it was forbidden for members of one tribe to speak to members of the other.

One year, on the night of the first full moon after the harvest, a baby was born in each of these tribes. In the tribe to the north it was a girl, daughter of the chief. He named her Moon Glow, for the first natural beauty he saw after gazing at her face for the first time. In the tribe to the south it was a male child, son of a mighty warrior. His father named him White Eagle, after the great bird which had soared majestically above his home at the moment of his son's birth.

When Moon Glow was fifteen, she was betrothed to her father's bravest warrior. As a wedding gift, she chose to make him a cloak of pure white leather, embroidered with eagle feathers in the image of a bison—his totem. She traveled from her village to find the most perfect feathers for the cloak.

At that time, White Eagle was being prepared for the rigors of war. His elders had sent him out in the mountains with only his clothes, his knife, and a flint to make fire. He had to live alone and survive for half the life of the moon—

*two weeks—with only those tools. He could not see any-
body or talk to anybody until he had completed his test.
While others before him had died alone and in shame,
White Eagle was determined to survive. In the wilderness
he had made the weapons of survival—a bow and many
arrows, even a spear. He had eaten well, he had slept
warmly. He was sure he would survive his test.*

*White Eagle had been in the mountains for ten days. His
only companion was a white stallion who roamed the
mountains near his camp.*

Suddenly Lisa sat upright. John was talking about
Kate's horse, the stallion they'd seen earlier! She listened closely as he went on.

*The horse ran whenever White Eagle tried to touch him
or capture him, but he seemed to like being near White
Eagle. The brave knew that the horse was wild, now and
forever, and somehow the horse's very wildness was a comfort to him.*

*One day Moon Glow walked in the mountains alone,
hunting for an eagle from whom she could pluck feathers for
the cloak. She did not see the mountain lion who stalked
her, nor did she hear him. But the mountain lion saw her.
Without warning, he attacked, howling and shrieking in
victory as he landed on her back. Moon Glow screamed,
knowing it would do no good and hearing in response only
the slow, sad echo of her own voice.*

White Eagle heard the cry of the mountain lion and leapt up from his fire. Then he heard the cry of Moon Glow and he ran. He was only vaguely aware of the presence of the white stallion—a shadow at his side in his flight toward destiny.

When he found Moon Glow and the mountain lion, the girl was struggling bravely against the overpowering force of the wild creature. Without hesitation, White Eagle drew an arrow from his quiver, slipped it into his bow, drew it back, and let it fly. But he had drawn too quickly. The first arrow sped right past the lion and the girl and struck the ear of the white horse who watched from beyond. The horse flinched momentarily, but stood his ground bravely as the arrow passed right through his ear and landed harmlessly beyond him. Then White Eagle shot again, taking more careful aim. His arrow met its target. The mountain lion fell limp and dead. White Eagle ran to Moon Glow and took her up in his arms. She was almost unconscious and bleeding badly. White Eagle knew she was near death.

All thoughts of himself fled from his mind. He knew only that he must save this woman and the only way he could save her would be to return her to her people. He did not think of the consequences; he thought only of the woman who needed him. He began the long walk to the north, carrying the chieftain's dying daughter in his arms.

As he walked, White Eagle became aware that the wild white stallion walked with him. It surprised him because it *was White Eagle's arrow that had wounded the stallion, but the ear showed no blood—just a nick that looked like an old wound, long healed. The stallion matched the brave step for step, never straying more than a few feet. And when a rock in the mountain caused White Eagle to stumble, the horse was there for White Eagle to lean on. It was the first time White Eagle had ever touched the horse. He was certain the horse would flee from his touch, but the stallion did not. He waited. Then White Eagle understood. The horse was offering to carry them to the north.*

*White Eagle lifted himself and Moon Glow onto the stallion's back. He cradled her in his arms as the sleek stallion made the journey.*

*It was an arduous journey, for Moon Glow had traveled far to search for feathers. When they arrived at her village, the chief took his daughter, but would not speak to White Eagle. The chief recognized him immediately as a son of the tribe of the south. White Eagle knew that his thanks was his life. He returned to the mountains.*

*Time passed. Moon Glow healed and White Eagle survived in the rest of his test. But neither could forget the other.*

*Then, one day, the stallion mysteriously appeared at White Eagle's village and seemed to invite White Eagle to ride on him. White Eagle climbed onto the horse's sleek back. The stallion took off immediately. Soon White Eagle found himself in the mountains once again. This time he* was not alone. Moon Glow was waiting there for him. She was well and beautiful. At the moment they saw one another, they knew that they would love each other for eternity and that the stallion understood their love and had brought them together.

Many times after that, the stallion carried the lovers to one another. Moon Glow delayed her marriage by insisting that she finish the cloak she was making for her future husband. She sewed the feathers on the soft, white leather, but try as she did to make it the pattern of a bison, it was an eagle, soaring gracefully. Though she knew she was being disloyal to her father and to her tribe, Moon Glow loved the design she had crafted, as she loved the man it stood for. She would present the cloak to White Eagle, rather than to her future husband.

Finally the day came that Moon Glow and White Eagle had always dreaded. On the day that Moon Glow planned to give the finished cloak to White Eagle, Moon Glow's future husband trailed the white horse to the mountains. When he found the lovers together, the warrior was angry and jealous. Hatred for this enemy of his people filled his heart. Vowing that the pair would be punished, he seized them both, bound their hands, and made them walk back to the village in shame. There was no sign of the white stallion as they walked. There would be no rescue this time.

The chief was shocked to learn of his daughter's treason. He immediately condemned White Eagle to death and

*offered his daughter to any of his braves who would still
have her.*

"Oh, that's so sad," Stevie interrupted. "How could
her father be so cruel!"
The others nodded as John continued.

*All hope was lost for the lovers. There was no escape for
either, and to both death seemed preferable to separation.
At the moment of White Eagle's execution, Moon Glow
swallowed some poison. She lived long enough to watch the
flames consume her beloved White Eagle and the flowing
white cloak he wore to his death. As the smoke drifted up to
the pale blue sky, she saw the distinct outline of a soaring
eagle take flight. She gasped—whether in pain or surprise,
nobody knows.*
*Then, at that moment, there was a thunder of hoof-
beats. A pure white stallion came galloping through the
village. He paused at the weak and dying Moon Glow.
With her last ounce of energy, she reached upward,
clutched the stallion's mane, and was swept up off the
ground. Magically the horse rose in the air and flew sky-
ward. Then, as the tribe watched, there appeared behind
her on the horse, the pure white leather cloak she had so
painstakingly made. On it was the perfect image of an
eagle.*

"The lovers are gone now," John said. "Living together in eternity. But they say the horse still roams the wilderness, riderless, on an endless quest to help others whose love transcends hatred and bigotry. He carries the nick in his ear as a reminder of White Eagle's sacrifice, for the moment the brave performed the selfless act of saving Moon Glow, his fate was sealed. Our people call the horse after him—White Eagle."

Without another word, John rose and left the room.

"WHO WAS THAT boy?" Christine asked, sighing.

"John," Stevie said. "He works here. Wasn't that a *romantic* story!"

"Imagine—a flying horse!" agreed Carole.

"My mother has told me a story sort of like that," Christine said. "Only she didn't tell it as well as John does. You know how important the traditional tales are to Native Americans don't you? The generations learn from one another as stories are passed through the ages. We were telling stories long before the Europeans figured out how to write them down!"

"Well, that guy really knows how to make up a good tale and tell it just right," Stevie said. "That's the sort of thing you learn at your parents' knees."

"Jealous?" Carole teased.

"No. He's not as good as I am, but he is good. I mean, his story did make me shiver, but not the way my story scared you guys, right?"

"His wasn't supposed to be a scary story," Carole said.

"Oh, yes it was," said Lisa, speaking for the first time. "It was meant to scare Kate from adopting the stallion."

"I know. And it's not fair," Kate added.

All four girls looked at Kate, suddenly aware how much John's romantic tale had touched her.

"I want that horse. I don't know how he knows that I do, but he does. And now he's trying to make me change my mind. I just don't know why."

"Maybe he wants the stallion himself," Lisa suggested.

"But how did he know *I* wanted it?"

Lisa gulped uncomfortably. "I told him," she confessed. "See, he asked me about the ride we took, and I mentioned the stallion. He seemed all upset about it at the time, but he wouldn't tell me why. I asked him if he wanted the stallion himself, and he said that wasn't it. He just said that nobody could have the stallion with the nick in his ear. It was strange. One minute he was friendly and helpful. The next minute he was all strange about the horse."

A confused look crossed Christine's face. "Wait. I know him. Isn't that Walter Brightstar's son, John?"

"Yes," Kate told her.

"Oh, there's something odd about them, isn't there? I mean, I sort of remember some kind of rumor. . . ."

"They're really good with horses," Lisa said, suddenly wanting to defend John. "When I saw John, he was staying with a mare who is going to foal soon. He said she was restless and seemed to like his company. She did, too. She finally fell asleep while he was there."

All four of Lisa's friends looked at her. "When was this?" Stevie asked.

"After supper," Lisa explained. "I went back out to the barn to get my watch. John was there with the mare."

"Ah, a late-night meeting in the barn! Just *happened* to forget your watch?" Stevie teased.

"It wasn't exactly late night," Lisa said. "It was seven-thirty. And, yes, I did just happen to forget my watch. Give me a break!"

Stevie regarded her carefully and then shrugged her shoulders. "Well, you're *probably* telling the truth," she said. She was teasing and Lisa knew it. "But I think John was just being a practical joker. He's a pretty funny guy. I'll bet he just happened to be passing by the bunkhouse and heard my story, then couldn't resist the opportunity to join in on the Halloween fun so he made up that fantastic ghost story."

"I don't think he made it up," Christine said. "As I told you, my mother used to tell me one very much like it. The people around here know lots and lots of Native American tales. They're mythical and romantic. Sometimes they're pretty hard to understand."

"This one wasn't," Kate said. "At least John's reason for telling it wasn't hard to understand. It was carefully designed to make me change my mind about owning the stallion. And all I can say is that it won't work."

"Well, I'll tell you one thing," Carole said. "It may be a story, but it certainly isn't true. Remember that John began it by saying it all happened before his own grandfather's memory? That means it must have happened at least seventy years ago, and most horses die in their twenties, though a few live to thirty, maybe thirty-five. There is no way a horse is going to live as long as seventy years! Out of the question."

"It's a story, Carole!" Stevie said. "It wasn't meant to be taken literally. Besides, if the story is correct, the silvery stallion is some kind of ghost anyway. Ghosts don't have ages the way people or horses do. They just exist. Sort of."

"Oh, I suppose," Carole conceded. "I was just trying to make Kate feel better."

"Thanks, Carole," Kate said. "You did make me feel

better. You and Stevie reminded me that John's story is just a story, and I don't have to pay any attention to it. I'm going to get that horse at the adoption, and now I know what I'm going to name him."

"Yes?" Stevie asked expectantly.

"White Eagle, of course."

With that, Kate reached for a marshmallow and speared it with a long-handled fork. She held it over the flames in the fireplace. It marked the end of the discussion as far as she was concerned. In a show of agreement and support, her friends followed suit. Soon five marshmallows were toasting over the fire, and Christine took over the job of tale teller.

Later that night, cuddled into her down sleeping bag, Lisa thought about all the things that had happened that day and tried to make sense of them.

First, there was the stallion. She could still see him rising above his herd of mares. He was simply magnificent—wild and free. Lisa wondered if he would be any less magnificent with a saddle and rider on his back. Was he so beautiful because he was free? That was a silly idea, of course. All the horses who roamed the country were descended from domesticated ponies, who had originally been brought to this country by the Spaniards who first explored and settled these lands. A horse that was beautiful free would also be beautiful under saddle, especially if he was lucky enough to have a rider as good as Kate Devine to own and ride him.

Then there was John. And there was John's story. Lisa knew she needed to think about John's story, but first she just wanted to think about John. He wasn't like anybody she'd ever met before. She liked that about him. At the same time, it frightened her a little bit. He was handsome, to be sure, but that wasn't what frightened her. He seemed like at least two different boys at once. He was the kind, gentle, caring young man who sat with a mare for hours, watching and comforting her when his own father should have been doing it. That gave Lisa a start. Just where had Walter been while all this was going on? He *should* have been the one with the mare. Was John covering for him? Lisa decided not to think about that right then, either.

Then there was the other John. That was the mysterious John who wasn't going to tell why Kate shouldn't adopt the stallion. That same John was the one who had shown up at the bunkhouse, walked in uninvited (it was a good thing they were all wearing sweatpants and sweatshirts to sleep in!), told a confusing and probably untrue story clearly designed to make Kate change her mind about owning the stallion, and then just walked out. What was he trying to do? More important, why was he trying to do it?

Lisa's mind replayed her conversations with John,

especially the story he'd told. In her mind she heard it over and over again. Finally she fell asleep with the image of the horse rising into the sky above the village, carrying the star-crossed lovers to their destiny. The image was to remain with her for a very long time.

## 6

"IF ONE MORE person asks me if they're going to have to peel the grapes, I'll scream," Stevie announced.

Lisa laughed. Stevie was pretending to be angry, but the fact was she was in her element. All five of the girls were at the regional high school, where the basement had been turned over to them for the party that was to take place tomorrow. Students from the school wandered in and out during their free periods, offering to help decorate or otherwise get ready. Kate and Christine had special dispensation from their own schools to have the time off to put together the Halloween Fair—as long as they got their homework in on time and got the notes they missed from classmates.

"Don't worry about your homework," Stevie told

them. "That's one of the things The Saddle Club is the very best at."

"You mean you're going to do it for me?" Kate asked, teasing.

"No, not me," Stevie assured her. "If I did it, you'd both flunk out. No, the one who does the best homework is Lisa. She can do anything!"

"Ahem," Lisa said. "She can also follow instructions. Like I'll be glad to help anybody with their homework. I don't *do* other people's work."

"Whatever," said Stevie. "Just don't worry. We'll come through for you."

"You always have," Christine said. "And that's what you're doing now, right?"

Stevie looked down. She was standing on top of a very tall ladder. "Actually," she said, "at this moment I'm not so sure." In one hand she had some orange crepe paper, and in the other was a piece of tape. The problem was she was going to have to put the two of them together on a spot she could reach. The best she could do was the edge of a fluorescent lamp.

"Okay?" she asked. Lisa was standing on the floor, holding the ladder to steady it.

"Sort of," Lisa told her. "But you'd better hurry down now. Two more people want to know who's going to peel the grapes."

"Yeooooooo!" Stevie said. But she was laughing

when she got back down to ground level. "I think I've got an idea," she said to Lisa, her eyes sparkling. That was usually a sign of a really good or a really bad idea. With Stevie it was sometimes hard to tell which was which. "The next person who asks me about the grapes will be assigned the job of putting up the rest of the crepe paper."

John Brightstar sauntered into the basement. "Hey, good morning, girls!" he greeted them. "The ninth grade has a free period, and my teacher said I should offer to help. Any grapes need peeling?"

Stevie blinked in astonishment. "No," she said sweetly. "But we have another job that's right up your alley. Come on aboard."

It turned out that John was actually the perfect person for the job of hanging orange and black crepe paper, because he was tall enough to reach the ceiling from the top of the ladder. It also meant that Lisa was assigned to retain her position of holding the ladder and steadying it. She held on very tightly.

Stevie didn't waste a second. There was an awful lot of work to do and it didn't seem as if there were anywhere near enough time to do it. Stevie mustered her troops to the area she'd designated as the horror house and began partitioning it off.

One section was where the awful things to feel—including the peeled grapes that blindfolded visitors would be told were eyeballs—would be laid out. Stevie knew that peeling grapes was a boring job, but she thought she and the girls could do it that night in the kitchen at The Bar None. After all, they'd just need a few of them. What was the big deal? They'd also cook the pasta designated as brains and fill long oiled balloons with water and tell everyone they were entrails. Stevie was pretty sure they could think of some more disgusting things before the fair, too. She just had to put her mind to it.

"Okay, this is where we're going to have the wind tunnel. Can anybody get their hands on a tube-type vacuum cleaner so we can reverse the air flow?"

Two hands went up. That solved that problem. It also gave Stevie two volunteers to run their own mothers' vacuum cleaners, since Stevie was pretty sure the mothers would insist on it anyway.

"And next comes the ghost mirror," Stevie said. "Is there a full-length mirror we can paint stuff on?"

There was. One of the high school students "borrowed" it from the girls' room upstairs, and Stevie assigned an aspiring art student the job of painting a suggestive ghost on it. That way, the "guest" in the horror house would see herself or himself, *plus* a ghost. Anyone who pooh-poohed the ghost would be treated to the immediate appearance of somebody dressed in an identical outfit.

"It's going to be great!" Stevie said. "Just make sure the ghost you paint is just a little wispy. We don't want anybody to be able to see anything clearly. The kids' imaginations are going to be doing an awful lot of work."

"Got it!" the artist said, and then disappeared to "borrow" some paints from the art room.

"Next, we have to have something for the kids to fall down on that won't hurt them."

"Mattresses?" somebody suggested.

"Probably," Stevie said. "But I'm open to other suggestions."

"Rubber balls? We've got a ton of them in the gym."

"We'd really need a ton of them," Stevie said. "I mean, this has to be safe. In spite of what the kids think, we have to treat them like precious packages. We want them scared, not hurt."

"You mean precious packages, like fragile things you ship places?" a redheaded boy asked. Stevie had the feeling he was on to something.

"Yes, very fragile," Stevie agreed. "What's on your mind?"

"Well, my father runs this mail-order business, and he just got a truckload—and I mean truckload—of Styrofoam peanuts. He uses them all right, but he doesn't use that many, and it's a three-year supply. The place that delivered them doesn't want to take them back. You getting the picture?"

"Perfect!" Stevie declared. "I'm sure he can get a tax deduction for a donation to a worthy cause. . . ."

"Probably, but I think he'll be happy enough just to get them out of the backyard. My mom won't mind, either."

"I hereby declare you in charge," Stevie said. "And we'll set that up over here. . . ."

There was so much to do, and it was all so much fun, that the girls barely noticed as the hours passed. By midafternoon, it seemed that Stevie had everybody in town—and certainly everybody in the school—jumping at her commands. Phyllis Devine pitched in and beamed proudly to see how well her team—The Saddle Club—was running the fair she was in charge of.

"Phyllis, you're brilliant," the principal of the school said, admiring how well everybody was working together. "I can't get these kids to work like this to put on a dance for themselves, much less to put together a Halloween Fair for little ones. What's your secret?" he asked.

"My magic ingredient?" She shrugged. "Hard to explain, but it all has to do with horses."

Since there wasn't a horse in sight (Carole was working on the pony rides *outside* the school), the principal couldn't make any sense out of Phyllis's remark. It didn't get any clearer when Stevie, Lisa,

Kate, and Christine all started laughing, either. The confused principal returned to his office, where he could fill out some more forms.

By four o'clock it was time to call it a day. They could finish up everything the following morning before the fair actually began. Surveying the work they'd done, though, they could hardly believe they'd only begun that morning. In a mere six or seven hours they'd taken a perfectly normal school basement and rec room and turned it into a total disaster area. Crepe paper hung from every possible place, curtains had been set up to divide the horror house into its components, including a hiding place for the reverse vacuumers and a ramp that would lead to the sea of Styrofoam, and tables had been strewn everywhere. Only Stevie knew which activity would be on which table. For now it just looked like a mess.

Stevie put her hands on her hips and admired the room filled with half-finished projects. "Isn't it just beautiful?" she asked. Only good friends would agree. They did.

"Okay, so what's next?" Lisa asked. She stifled a yawn. She was tired from holding the ladder all afternoon.

"Next is costumes," Stevie said.

"Wait a minute, we know what we're going to be," Carole reminded her. "We're going to be mice."

"Sure, but that doesn't mean there isn't any work to do. We have to figure out how to make ears and check that we've got the makeup we need for our whiskers. There's a lot left to do. We can't waste a minute."

"My mother promised me she'd help me with my costume tonight," Christine said. "I'll bet she can make six mouse ears in no time at all. Why don't you come to my house?"

"Can she do a farmer's wife?" Kate asked, suddenly inspired. After all, if her best friends were going to be the three blind mice, the least she could do was join them.

"In a New York minute," Christine promised. "Actually, I think she's got a gingham dress and an apron already. She might have to take the dress in a little, or else stuff it—oh, come on home with me and let's see what she can do. In any case, you all will have a chance to see the adobe dollhouse."

"Great," Stevie said. "I'm really dying to see it."

It took the girls a few minutes to tidy up a few (very few) things so they would know where to begin the next day. Stevie, Lisa, and Carole had each brought their basic mouse outfits—gray sweatpants and hooded sweatshirts—assuming that they'd end up at the store in town to look for something to make ears from. The fact that Mrs. Lonetree might be able to help them was awfully good news. She was a very creative person and probably would make better mouse ears than they could ever hope to!

The best news, though, was that getting there was going to be half the fun. The girls had ridden their horses into town that morning and had let them loose in a corral the high school maintained for the students who rode to school. Now they would ride to Christine's house and eventually back to The Bar None. That was always a pleasant prospect, but now all the more so since it was quite dark outside.

Stevie gave a final tug to the cinch on Stewball's saddle and climbed aboard. "It's a good thing horses can see in the dark," she said. "Because I don't think I can see a thing."

"Don't be so sure," Christine told her. "Once your eyes adjust to the darkness, you'll be surprised how much you can see—especially since there are a lot of stars out tonight."

"And the moon?" Lisa asked, looking to the sky.

"It's not up yet," Christine said. "But when it comes out, it should be nice, because it's almost full. I love riding by moonlight."

"Me, too," Carole said. She climbed into the saddle. "Actually, that's an understatement," she continued. "The fact is that I love riding anywhere, anytime. That includes by moonlight."

"Me, too," Kate said. Then she asked, "Everybody ready?"

They were, and they were off. Christine led the way since she knew the route to her own house the best. At first the girls followed the road out of town. They knew that they could take the road all the way to the Lonetrees' house, but the fact was that it was going to be a lot more fun to leave the roadway and cut across the open land. Their journey was aided then by the fact that the moon rose at the moment they left the road. It stood on the horizon, nearly full, big, orange, and bright. It almost seemed to lay a path for them to follow.

"This way," Christine said. It was easy to see where they were going. It was a fun ride.

Even though each girl was quite aware of the fact that they were in the twentieth century, not far from things like power plants and gas stations and a school with no fewer than two computer labs, it somehow seemed to each of them as if they had left all that behind. Every step into the open countryside felt like a step back in time, away from electronics and nuclear power, away from microwaves and dishwashers. The years dropped off as a snake sheds its skin. Lisa found herself thinking about life in the Old West, wondering what it would have been like just to survive. Stevie's mind turned to images of cowboys and stagecoaches, just as she'd seen in so many movies. Carole found herself thinking about the animals that had once wandered so freely and so safely on the land. Christine thought of her own family's people, part of the original American West. Kate thought about the horses, brought here from Europe, allowed to roam free—the magnificent animals who ruled the prairies and the desert lands.

*How-oooooooo!*

Even though the girls from Virginia had never heard that sound before, they knew instantly what it was. It was unmistakable. It was a coyote.

"Watch it!" Christine warned.

The girls all drew their horses to a halt. They listened again. The coyote howled again.

*How-oooooooo!*

He was a good distance from them, so they knew they weren't in any immediate danger, but the fact that there was one coyote around could mean that there were more. Coyotes didn't usually attack humans. Still, they were dangerous animals, and it made sense for the girls to hurry on their way.

"Okay, let's go," Christine said.

"No, wait!" Kate said, staying still. "Look!"

The girls looked where she pointed. The object of the coyote's call became apparent then, as a cloud of dust rose from the dry earth to the south of where they waited.

"It's the herd," Carole said. "The horses! They must have been startled by the coyote. Look at them."

While the motionless horses had been nearly invisible to the girls' eyes, the moving herd was very apparent. The mares and their young were milling frantically and simply making their presence more apparent to all the creatures around, especially the coyotes.

"We've got to help them!" Carole said.

"By doing what?" Christine asked. "What's going on here is what's been going on for thousands of years. There's nothing for us to do."

"But the coyotes—they could attack the horses!" Carole couldn't bear the idea that one of the herd might serve as dinner for the coyotes.

"The horses can take care of themselves," Kate said. Her eyes didn't move from the scene in front of her.

Her friends watched as well. Then the entire scene was dimmed when a cloud swept across the sky, obscuring the big, round orange moon. Suddenly there was only darkness.

*How-ooooooooo!*

All motion among the horses stopped as abruptly as it had started. After a moment of stillness, there was movement in the center of the pack, where a silvery stallion ran in circles and whinnied loudly. There was something else about him, something odd. Lisa squinted.

"Did you see that?" She couldn't believe what her eyes were telling her, but there appeared to be a white-clad figure on the stallion's back.

"What was it?"

The horse shifted directions again and began a gallop to safety. Unquestioning, the brood followed his lead. Within seconds the whole herd began to disappear behind an outcrop of rocks.

"It was a rider," Kate said breathlessly, sitting forward in her saddle for a clearer view of the now almost invisible herd.

"Don't be silly—" Carole said, dismissing the claim.

"Pure silvery white, just like the horse," Lisa said.

"And just like White Eagle—" Christine added.

"Oh, come on you guys," Stevie said. "It's just John, playing another joke on us."

"Do you think—?" Kate began.

"Of course I do," Stevie said. "You don't really believe in ghosts, do you?"

Kate closed her eyes and shook her head as if trying to shake the image from her mind. Then she opened her eyes again. "I don't suppose so," she said. "You're probably right, it was John."

"Well, more power to him," Carole said. "At least

he figured out how to save the horses from being attacked by the coyotes."

"I don't think that was what he had in mind when he planned the joke," Kate said. "I think he was just trying to scare me away again."

"I don't think we're going to get anywhere trying to know what's going on in John Brightstar's mind," Christine said. "Let's just get to my house."

The girls proceeded together. The thoughts of pioneer days were gone now for Lisa. The only thing on her mind was John. Maybe Kate was right—he was trying to scare her off—but Lisa had to admit that that was a pretty incredible thing to do. Not only was he the kind of boy who would take care of an ailing horse and come up with a deliciously romantic tale to justify keeping a horse in the wild, he'd even risk riding the creature!

Or was it possible, just possible, that John's story was true and the stallion had come to help them because they were helping the children on the Indian reservation?

Lisa really didn't know what to think. All she knew was that she had a lot to think about. And his name was John.

MRS. LONETREE WAS positively a whiz with her sewing machine. Within what seemed like a matter of minutes, she'd created three adorable sets of mouse ears— field mice, not Mickey—and had them tacked onto the girls' sweatshirt hoods.

"They're perfect," Lisa declared, and everybody agreed.

Then she deftly unfolded three wire coat hangers and quickly covered them with white felt. The blind mice now had canes to walk with. The final touch would be sunglasses, and Mrs. Lonetree said the girls were just going to have to do that themselves. Lisa, Stevie, and Carole thought that was more than fair. Then, while Mrs. Lonetree was adjusting the old gingham dress to create a farmer's-wife outfit for Kate, Christine took the "mice" into the bathroom, where they could all practice applying whiskers with an eyebrow pencil.

"Should they curl?" Stevie asked.

"I don't think so," Lisa said. By then, though, it was too late for Stevie. Her whiskers curled all the way up to her eyebrows!

"This is just a test," Stevie reminded her friends, working hard to remove the pencil marks. "I mean, we're supposed to make our mistakes now, aren't we?"

Lisa and Carole giggled and tried their own whiskers. In the end it turned out that the best ones were just a few brief straight lines radiating from above their mouths. Soon they each had proper whiskers and assured Stevie that her unsuccessful curly whiskers were hardly visible anymore.

"Nothing a shower and a scrub-brush and some bathroom cleanser can't get off," Stevie agreed cheerfully.

"Very nice," Christine said, admiring the results of the girls' efforts. "Would you like your cheese now or later?"

"That realistic?" Lisa asked.

"Absolutely, and if you think you look good, wait until you see how Kate is looking."

When they returned to Mrs. Lonetree's workroom,

they were astonished. It was their friend Kate, all right, but she didn't look at all as she had a mere fifteen minutes ago. She was wearing a very well-padded gingham dress with a long skirt and a full apron. She had a white cap on her head and a very long carving knife in one hand. Mrs. Lonetree said her outfit would be complete with the addition of some black leather shoes.

"I think this particular farmer's wife is going to have to make do with black leather riding boots. Will it work?"

"It will be the perfect touch," Mrs. Lonetree agreed. Then she turned to Christine. "So what's it to be for you?" she asked.

"Mine's going to take a little longer," Christine said. "Can we work on it later?"

"Sure," her mother agreed. "That will give me some time now to show the girls the dollhouse."

"Oh, thank you!" Stevie said. "I was afraid you wanted to keep it a surprise. Where is it?"

"This way," Mrs. Lonetree said, standing up from her sewing machine. She took the girls into her pottery studio. They had seen her work before. It was very special and very beautiful. Some shelves had pots that she was making for tourists. She followed the authentic traditional shapes and designs. The ones she was prouder of, however, were more modern interpretations of the traditional Native American pots. Carole and Lisa looked to see the new items she was working on. Lisa had taken pottery lessons for a while and had an idea of how difficult the work was. She really admired Mrs. Lonetree's skill. She was about to say so when the first gasp of delight came from Stevie, whose eyes had gone straight to the dollhouse.

"Oh, wow!" Stevie said, hurrying to where the dollhouse stood.

Carole and Lisa joined her and agreed with her completely.

There, in the middle of the studio, was the dollhouse. It was a perfect model of an adobe pueblo—a Southwest Native American home. A pueblo was essentially a box with steps on one side leading to the flat roof. There was only one entrance to the pueblo and that was from the top, via ladder. Since this was a dollhouse, Mrs. Lonetree had designed it so the whole thing opened in the center with a hinge to reveal the inside.

There were simple furnishings with traditional designs and patterns. A shelf near the cooking area held a complete array of miniature pots and bowls—just like the ones Mrs. Lonetree made for the tourists. There was a wall hanging, a woven rug, in traditional patterns. A rough-hewn table held miniature weapons used by the Native Americans of the old days—

knives, a bow, and even some very tiny arrows that actually had feathers on the shafts!

There were small wooden cooking utensils as well as gardening tools.

"It's perfect!" Stevie said.

"How can you bear to give it away?" asked Lisa.

Mrs. Lonetree smiled. "I had fun making it," she said. "Now somebody should have fun playing with it. I suppose I *could* have made some dolls, but . . ."

"Don't even think of it," Stevie said. "You've already done about a hundred times more than anybody could possibly ask. And if you want to know what I think, I think donating this incredibly beautiful work of art to benefit the after-school program at the reservation school is just about perfect."

"I kind of thought the same thing," Mrs. Lonetree said. "Those kids need every bit of help they can get. So, with your clever planning and my pots and sewing machine, we'll do well by them, won't we?"

"The best we can," Stevie said.

Lisa had a little chill right then. From the moment she'd heard about the Halloween Fair, she'd always known that it was for a good cause. Hearing how strongly Mrs. Lonetree felt made it seem even more important. It was one thing to know that you were involved in a good cause. It was another to understand, truly, that real people were going to get real benefit from it. Knowing how much work, love, and pride Mrs. Lonetree was giving to their efforts on behalf of the after-school program made Lisa see her entire trip out West in a much clearer light. She felt even better about herself and her friends.

The girls would have liked to have stayed at the Lonetrees', maybe even have a chance to play with the dollhouse a bit, but Kate reminded them that her mother was counting on their help serving dinner, and they had to get back to The Bar None.

The girls packed up their costumes, put them in their saddlebags, and got ready for the trip back home. They all thanked Mrs. Lonetree profusely for her help—in every possible way—and they remounted their horses for the final leg of their journey.

The Bar None was a short distance, perhaps two miles, across country from the Lonetrees' house. It was a trip the girls, especially Kate, had made many times, in dark and daylight. They felt safe and sure about their journey.

It had been a long and busy day, following an even longer and busier day. They rode together without talking, just enjoying the journey and thinking how welcome a good meal and a warm bunk were going to be very soon.

Lisa loved the countryside. At first look it had seemed barren to her, but now she knew better. The rocks and mountains were home for many creatures who managed to make meals of the brush and cactus that covered the land. Part of the trail back to The Bar None led through what felt like a gully between two craggy hills. One of those hills rose nearly straight up from the desert floor. A movement at the top of it caught Lisa's eye. She looked up. There, standing on a flat area at the edge of the hill, was the stallion, now clearly riderless. His herd was not in sight. He was completely silhouetted by the moonlight that streamed from behind him.

Lisa drew her horse to a halt to look, just look. Around her, her friends did the same, for they'd all seen him at the same moment.

The stallion rose then, rearing regally on his hind legs. His forelegs pawed eagerly at the vast expanse of sky in front of him. A breeze lifted his mane, brushing it back. The sight took Lisa's breath away.

The horse landed back on all fours. Without hesitation he turned around and disappeared down the other side of the hill.

"You've just *got* to have him," Stevie said.

Kate nodded, unable to speak.

CHOCOLATE HAD PICKED up a stone in her shoe on the way back from Christine's. Lisa had to get it out, or the horse's hoof would be tender and painful by morning.

Stevie, Carole, and Kate hurried to help Phyllis serve dinner while Lisa worked at Chocolate's hoof with the pick.

She'd removed plenty of stones and usually thought of it as a sort of a challenge. As long as her horse wasn't upset, Lisa was willing to work away at it. Chocolate seemed to understand completely that Lisa was doing this for her benefit. She didn't even flinch while Lisa tried to dig under the stone.

"Need help?"

Lisa looked up to find John standing there.

"No, I think I can do it," she said. "It's just that this stone is lodged in there something awful. It's Chocolate who may need help."

John stood by the mare's head and began patting her. She seemed to welcome the assurance.

"There's a sharp point on the stone, and it's stuck in a ridge or something in the shoe. The only good news here is that the part that's pushing on Chocolate's foot is round and smooth. All I need to do then is to"—she gritted her teeth, grunted, shifted the angle of the pick, and worried it back around the stone—"get this thing just so that"—she had it; she eased the handle of the pick until she felt the resistance of the stone, then with a swift and smooth motion she flexed the tool—"the stone will"—it popped out—"pop out," she said proudly.

"Nice work," John said.

Lisa lowered Chocolate's foot and patted the mare affectionately. Chocolate regarded her and then blinked. Lisa was pretty sure that was as close as she was going to get to a thank-you from Chocolate. "You're welcome," she told the horse. Then she unhooked the lead rope from Chocolate's halter and slapped her flank gently, telling the mare it was time to run free—until tomorrow. Chocolate obeyed willingly.

Lisa turned to John, then, though she didn't really know what to say to him. This boy had a way of turning up when she least expected him.

"You did a good job with the crepe paper this afternoon," she said. That sounded pretty lame to her, but it was the best she could come up with right then.

"Yeah, and you did a wonderful job holding the ladder," he returned. She shrugged and blushed. It was clear that John wasn't the kind of boy who would let her get away with being lame. She wished she hadn't made the remark about the crepe paper, but it was too late to take it back, and John was on to something else.

"I want to show you something," he said. "Come with me."

Before she could say anything, he took her hand and led her into the barn. Lisa wasn't used to having a boy hold her hand. It gave her a nice chill and made her knees feel a little funny—a little off balance. John did seem to have a way of making her feel off balance no matter what he did.

"What is it?" she asked.

"Remember the mare?"

"Of course."

"The vet was wrong."

"About what?"

"About how long it would be until she foaled." John drew to a stop at the box stall where he had been sitting with the edgy mare just a little less than twenty-four hours earlier. The stall was still occupied, but now there was more than just a mare. There was a mare and a foal.

"Oh, when was it born?" she asked breathlessly.

"This afternoon. Isn't she a cute filly?"

Lisa nodded. The filly seemed to know that they were talking about her. She looked curiously at Lisa, her bright eyes taking in everything. Then she flicked her skinny little gray tail and turned all her attention to her mother. It was, after all, supper time.

"She's adorable!" Lisa said. "Thanks for showing her to me."

"I knew you'd love her."

Lisa crossed her forearms on the top of the door to the stall and put her chin on her wrist so she could watch the filly and the mare.

"You know, a newborn horse is an amazing creature," she observed. "They usually stand up within a few minutes of being born and walk almost immediately. When I compare that to how long it takes the average human to do those things, it's not hard to understand why horses are so much more fun to ride."

John laughed. "I never thought of it that way, but you're probably right."

"Were you here when she was born?" Lisa asked.

"I was," he said. "I'm glad I was, too. The mare didn't turn out to need any help, but I wanted to be here in case she did. The vet said she had more than a week to go, but I didn't think he was right."

"How did you learn so much about horses and foaling?" Lisa asked.

John seemed to hesitate, but he answered. "My mother was a horse breeder," he told her. "She taught me everything I know. It's part of the legacy she left me."

"Left you?" Lisa asked.

"She's dead," he said. And the way he said it warned Lisa she shouldn't ask any more. His tone of voice was like a door slamming in her face. This was the mystery, she recalled. It had something to do with John's mother. There probably was an answer, but Lisa wasn't going to get it from John. She was slightly annoyed that he trusted her so little. She wanted to change the subject, and she wanted to take the upper hand.

"We saw the stallion again tonight. Twice in fact."

"Still running free?"

"As you very well know," she said.

"Why should I know?" he asked. "I don't know when they round up the horses for the adoption."

"Very good," Lisa said. "Nice try. But we saw you. You were there when the coyotes were calling."

John looked puzzled. "When was that?" he asked.

"About four-thirty," Lisa said. "Just about exactly the same time you climbed on the stallion's back and rode him."

"Somebody was riding him?"

"Yes, John. We saw somebody—or some*thing*—mounted on the stallion."

John was silent for a moment. Then he spoke. "I've heard talk of incidents like that," he said.

"Come on, John," Lisa said. She was getting a little tired of his mysterious tale and wished he would just loosen up and tell her the truth. "We saw you."

"You saw somebody," he said. "I believe you. But you didn't see me. I was here. I came home on the school bus, and I never left the mare's side. The filly was born at five o'clock this afternoon."

Lisa looked at the filly, and she knew that John would never have abandoned that mare in the middle of foaling just to play a trick on some girls. No way.

Even later, after it was all over, Stevie and her friends couldn't believe how much work they got done by the time the fair opened. It seemed like a mad rush to finish everything, and Stevie wondered if they'd ever manage to get their own costumes on, but somehow they did it. At exactly eighteen seconds before noon on Saturday, they were ready. They were still breathless from the dash, but three blind mice and the farmer's wife all stood in line waiting for the first guests to arrive at the high school basement.

"Where's Christine?" Lisa asked.

"She's still getting dressed," Kate said. "She was very mysterious about her costume. All I know is that her mother seemed pleased with all the work she'd done."

"Greetings, girls." It was a boy's voice, but it was a man's costume. Stevie looked, gasped, and giggled. It had to be John, but there was no true way to recognize him. He was dressed as the headless horseman! He was wearing black jeans, black boots, and a very large black turtleneck that rose up over his head. Stevie suspected he was using one or two sets of football shoulder pads to hold it up, and the effect was really good. He'd also managed to find a black cloak with a bright red lining, which helped mask the slight oddity of his big, high shoulders and his relatively small, short arms.

"Has anybody seen my friend Ichabod?" he asked.

Lisa laughed. "I think he'll be here in a few minutes. Why don't you join us on the receiving line and scare the daylights out of all the kids who are about to arrive."

"Gladly," he said, standing next to her.

"You all have done a *wonderful* job," Phyllis Devine said in the moment of quiet before the storm when the doors would open. "I think we'll have a great financial success, but I know that, no matter what, we're going to be running a party here this afternoon that no child is going to forget. It wouldn't be the same without all the help you have given. So I want to thank you all— say, where's Christine?"

"I'm right here," she said, entering the room from behind them. When the girls turned to look, they were stunned. Christine Lonetree was dressed as the young Indian boy from the story that John had told. She was wearing a completely white outfit that was topped by a white cape. On the back of the cape Mrs. Lonetree had painted a flying eagle.

Lisa's eyes flitted to John, still standing next to her. She wondered what he thought. She couldn't see his face behind the long neck of his "headless" top, but she could hear his low whistle of admiration.

Before anybody could say anything, the doors flew open and young children filled the room. The rush was on!

CAROLE LOVED BEING in charge of pony rides. She was always happiest around any kind of a horse, but now it was even truer because the kids were having such fun. Most of these children were familiar with horses, so that made the job a lot easier. Even better, though, was the fact that they were all in costume and were having their pictures taken by Frank Devine. The pony was sporting a witch's pointed hat, and it seemed to go perfectly with the costume that each child wore—everything from the Incredible Hulk to Sleeping Beauty (snoring loudly). Carole saw to it that each child had a fun ride, got a good picture, and learned a new fact about horses.

"You tell their age by how their teeth have worn," she said to one rider.

"There's no such thing as a white horse, just gray, no matter how white the horse looks," another learned.

"English riders have their stirrups shorter than Western," one child heard.

"Horses don't have any nerves in their manes, so you can hold it for balance if you need to, and it won't hurt the horse. Of course, that's not good riding style, but it may be excellent safety sometime!"

All of the kids seemed to like what they were learning as well as what they were doing. Although Carole knew she wanted to work with horses for the rest of her life, she'd always thought her choices were among owner, breeder, trainer, and vet. Today she was having so much fun teaching, she was beginning to think she ought to add instructor to the list.

"Smile now," she told the Teenage Mutant Ninja Turtle in the saddle. Somewhere under the costume she was sure the child was smiling a lot.

"WHAT HAPPENED TO you?" Kate asked Christine.

"I think I just got trampled by two sugarplum fairies and a robot," Christine explained, rubbing her shoulder, which had gotten slightly bruised. "Those fairies were determined to get to the costume parade!"

Kate giggled.

When Christine's shoulder stopped throbbing, she laughed, too. "It means they're having a good time, and that's what this is about," she said philosophically. "At least I think that's what that means." She rubbed her shoulder again.

"What those two fairies don't know, however, is that you're one of the judges of the costume parade!"

"I am?"

"You are now," Kate said, tugging at Christine's cape. "And there's work to be done."

"OF COURSE IT'S your pumpkin, and you can do whatever you want," Phyllis Devine said to a teary-eyed ghost. "It doesn't matter what that vampire next to you says. If you want a happy pumpkin, you get a happy pumpkin."

"Really?"

"Really."

The ghost turned to the vampire and stuck her tongue out at him.

"JUST GUESS," STEVIE said. "You really can't possibly count all the candy corns just by looking at the jar. You're supposed to *guess*."

"Is it more than two thousand?" the panda in front of her asked.

"Guess," Stevie repeated. "Actually, you can guess as many times as you want. It only costs you a quarter for each guess, and the more guesses you make, the better chance you have of winning the dollhouse."

Once again Stevie pointed to the photograph of the adobe dollhouse that had been getting so much attention. The panda reached into her pocket and pulled out six tickets worth twenty-five cents each. Then she took six slips of paper, carefully wrote her name on the top of each, and wrote 2,000; 2,001; 2,002; 2,003; 2,004; and 2,005.

"I'm pretty sure it's more than two thousand," she told Stevie earnestly as she tucked her entry forms into the cigar box.

"I hope you win," Stevie said. She meant it, too.

MRS. LONETREE HANDED a clean paintbrush to Superman.

"You can paint whatever you'd like on our mural, but a lot of the children have chosen to paint themselves, in their costumes. I think a nice place for Superman would be—"

"Right here," he said, pointing to the top of the mural. "I can fly, you know."

"I know," said Mrs. Lonetree. "Let me get you a

chair to stand on so you can put yourself in just the right place!" She did that. She also brought him the red, blue, and yellow paints so he'd make himself the right colors. The mural, a piece of brown wrapping paper that was eight feet tall and twenty-five feet long, was taped to one very long wall of the basement. Anybody who wanted to was invited to come and paint anything they wanted on it. It was another one of Stevie's bright ideas, and it was working beautifully. The youngest kids weren't very good at drawing ghosts and goblins, but to most viewers' eyes, the scribbles of color were just as pretty as the neat ballerina next to them.

"Can I have some orange?" Superman asked.

"Sure," Mrs. Lonetree said. "What's going to be orange?"

"Oh, it's the sun that Superman is melting in order to be able to fry some bad guys who are trying to steal all the television sets in Metropolis so nobody can watch cartoons. . . ."

He was interrupted by a little girl. "Hey! Don't get your old sun all over my balloon that's supposed to be taking Dorothy back to Kansas!"

Superman promised to be careful.

Mrs. Lonetree smiled. This mural will be very special, she thought to herself as she went to fetch the orange paint.

*AAAAAAAARRRHHHHHH!*

It was a bloodcurdling scream—just exactly the kind everybody wanted to hear coming out of the horror house. It was immediately followed by joyful giggles.

"Don't do that again!" one child chided.

"What? I didn't do anything!"

"You didn't?"

That was the sort of conversation Lisa had been hearing ever since she'd taken her position behind the black curtain in the horror house. Her job was to reach out and tickle kids from behind after they'd passed her. They somehow always thought it had been done by whomever they were with.

"No," the companion said.

"You did *too!*"

Then she'd scoot up a bit, reach out, and tickle the other person.

"What was that?"

"It wasn't me!"

That was when Lisa would scream. It was more fun than she could remember having for a long time, and the best part of it was that the kids loved it, too. Usually by that time they'd figured out that they weren't alone, and they'd start laughing. Some of them could hardly walk because they were laughing so hard. Their enjoyment was a real tribute to Stevie. If Lisa had ever doubted it, she knew for sure now the truth of the notion that Stevie was a genius. Nobody else could have possibly come up with such a wonderfully scary and funny horror house as this. And that was before the kids even got to the part where the vacuum cleaners blew out at them, or where they landed on Styrofoam peanuts.

"Now follow me *this* way," came a familiar voice. It was John. He had volunteered to be a guide in the horror house. Each pair of children going through the house had a guide just to be sure they didn't get lost or too scared. Also, it was a way to guarantee that they wouldn't *counter*attack!

Lisa reached out at just the right minute and tickled one child. Then, as the argument got going between the visitors, she tickled the other. Pretty soon they were both laughing. The headless horseman seemed to turn in her direction, and if she hadn't been sure that she could not have possibly seen it, she would have sworn that the headless horseman had winked at her.

Once again she was struck by what an interesting mix of characteristics John Brightstar was. He had seemed so serious and distant last night, and now he was acting as if he didn't have a care in the world. She was so intrigued by her observations that she almost forgot to tickle a leprechaun.

IT FILLED STEVIE'S heart with joy to look at the over-stuffed cigar box of entries for the Kount the Kandy Korn Kontest. Mrs. Lonetree's dollhouse had brought every single child to the table. Several of the children had spent as long looking at the photograph as they had looking at the jar. Stevie particularly recalled two girls who had invented an imaginary family and had begun playing with them in the dollhouse just as they stood at the table. Whoever won it was going to be the happiest child in Two Mile Creek. Now all Stevie had to do was be sure that everybody who wanted to enter the contest had a chance and then figure out who had won.

No, she realized with a start. That *wasn't* all she had to do. She had to get the dollhouse as well. She felt the blood drain from her face. How could she have forgotten? Mrs. Lonetree had had to walk over this morning. Christine had ridden her horse. Neither could bring the dollhouse. Stevie had promised to call Frank and ask him to stop by the Lonetrees' and bring it on his way, but she'd completely forgotten. Now she was about to have a winner, and she didn't have a prize.

She'd spent too much time watching how excited the children were at the prospect of winning. After seeing those faces she couldn't tell the winner he or she was going to have to wait. Somehow she had to get the dollhouse back to the fair before the winner was announced—in exactly one hour.

Stevie looked around for help. Everybody was busy. Carole was still taking kids on rides. Mrs. Lonetree was up to her elbows in clay, showing a group of fascinated children how to make miniature bowls. Phyllis Devine was overseeing the cupcake decorating. Kate was turning masked kids in circles so they could pin the stem on the pumpkin, and Christine was doing something with two sugarplum fairies. Nobody could help Stevie. She was going to have to do this herself. But what was she going to do?

Stevie realized that Mr. Lonetree wasn't there. That probably meant he was at the ranch and would be able to drive the dollhouse over to the school. It wasn't a long distance. All she had to do was call.

She dug into her pocket, found change, and located the students' pay phone on the first floor of the school.

*I'm sorry. We are experiencing technical difficulties. Please try to place your call again later.*

She checked the number. She had it right. She tried again.

*I'm sorry. . . .*

For how long could there be technical difficulties?

*I'm sor—*

She couldn't wait. She didn't have time to wait. She

had to do something. The only thing she could think of was to go to the Lonetrees' house herself and hope that Mr. Lonetree would be there to bring her and the dollhouse back.

She tucked the quarter back into her pocket. She would ride Stewball there. She knew the way. It wouldn't take long. But she had to tell somebody what she was doing.

She found Christine standing outside the girls' bathroom.

"The sugarplum fairies had to go," she explained. "I'm waiting for them, and then I promised to take them through the horror house."

Stevie wasn't sure she understood exactly how Christine had gotten to be the girls' personal attendant at the fair, but Christine said it had something to do with a consolation prize for the costume parade. That made some sense—not much, but enough.

Stevie explained her dilemma. "Do you think your dad's at home?" she asked.

"I'm sure he will be," she said. "I'm also sure he'll drive you back. Too bad about the phones, but it happens. Do you know the trail?"

"Yes," Stevie assured her. "It's not hard to follow. I'm sure I'll be fine."

"I'm sure you will be, too. But it's going to be cold. Do you have a jacket?"

"No, just this sweatshirt," Stevie said.

"Well, it's not much, but here, take my cloak. It should help some with the breezes."

"Thanks," Stevie said, slipping the cloak over her shoulders. Then, when the girls'-room door opened, Stevie got a look at herself in the mirror. There she was, one blind field mouse, wearing a silvery white cloak. It seemed about right for a Halloween ride.

9

STEWBALL SHOOK HIS head and snorted. Stevie
thought that was his way of saying he was happy to be
out of the corral and out on a trail. Stevie agreed. It
was quite dark outside, and it was cool, but it was
pleasant. She leaned forward and patted the horse on
his neck just to show that she felt the same way. Then
she nudged him a little, and they began trotting.
Much as she was enjoying the ride, she didn't want to
be gone too long from the fair. Besides, she couldn't
wait to find out who won the adobe dollhouse.

There was a screeching sound. Stewball's ears flicked
eagerly. Stevie looked to where she'd heard the noise,
but saw nothing.

"It must have been some kind of bird or something,

boy," she told the horse. "I mean, just because it's Halloween . . ." Her voice trailed off.

It *was* Halloween. That was supposed to be a night when ghosts and ghouls roamed free. Witches flew through the sky, casting spells. Vampires ruled the blood supply. Headless horsemen thundered along roadways after unwary victims. It was a night of unfettered evil. . . .

"Oh, stop it," Stevie told herself. She spoke out loud as if trying to be sure she heeded her own words. "It's just another date on the calendar. There's nothing special about it. It's just the end of October and . . . and, uh . . ."

She saw something. She'd definitely seen something. Stewball felt her tense up and took it as a signal. He stopped. That wasn't what she wanted at all. She wanted to get out of there! She clicked her tongue and tapped him with her heels. He began walking again, very slowly. Stevie got a grip on herself and looked around cautiously.

She had left the road and was now crossing the open land. It was the same trail she'd followed with her friends just over twenty-four hours ago. But it didn't look the same at all. Now that she was alone, it didn't look beautiful and exciting. It looked barren and dangerous. Stevie shivered.

There was the screech again. She looked up to

where the sound had come from this time. A dark shadow passed across the full moon, which stood just above the horizon. Stevie sighed with relief. It was a bird, probably some kind of owl, since they were night hunters. It had a big wingspan to be sure, but it wasn't big enough to be a threat to Stevie or Stewball.

"Come on, boy. Let's just get this over with, okay?" They rode on.

There were the familiar landmarks. She spotted the promontory where they'd seen the stallion rear. It was still outlined by the bright moon. This time there was no sign of the stallion, and what had appeared as an interesting piece of landscape when she'd been with her friends now seemed to be merely stark. Her mind was flooded with an image of riding the stallion to the edge of the cliff. He reared, she held on tightly. His weight shifted. She grabbed his mane. His feet slipped. . . .

"Oh, stop it!" she said again.

Something grabbed her hair. She screamed, and Stewball started. Stevie managed to hold the reins, and the horse stopped. She flailed wildly to free her hair from the unearthly creature that held it, harder and tighter with every motion. The more she struggled, the harder it was—until Stewball took two steps backward. That was when the tension was released on the branch and Stevie's hair was freed. Still shaking, she looked over her shoulder to be sure. That's all it was—just a branch.

"I think we'd better get going," she said to Stewball. Without further ado, he picked up a trot. Stevie was beginning to get the feeling that this exciting solo night ride couldn't be over fast enough.

She needed something to give her courage and decided that the best something would be a distraction. She decided to try singing. Horses liked singing. Stewball would probably get courage from it, too. Also, Stewball wasn't likely to be much of a music critic, so he wouldn't care if she hit a wrong note. She knew just the song to sing for him.

*"Old Stewball was a racehorse,*
*And I wish he were mine.*
*He never drank water;*
*He always drank wi-ine!"*

She smiled at her choice. Not only was it good to sing a song about her very own horse, it was also a song with dozens of verses and would keep her mind and her voice occupied for miles.

*"His bridle was silver,*
*His mane it was gold.*

*And the worth of his saddle*
*Has never been to-old!*

*To-old!"*

Who was that? Stevie's heart jumped.
"Hello!"
*Hello!*
Her voice bounced back at her off the mountain-side.

"Oh, swell," Stevie said, disgusted with herself. "I've gotten so spooked that I'm fighting off branches and getting scared of a dumb old echo. Come on, Stewball. Let's get back to work." She took a deep breath and began singing again.

*"I bet on the gray mare,*
*I bet on the bay.*
*If I'd've bet on old Stewball,*
*I'd be a free man today!"*

It wasn't working. The singing didn't make her feel any better, and she knew that Stewball could feel her tension right through the saddle. If Stevie had learned one thing about horses, it was that you couldn't fool them. They knew when their riders knew what they were doing. If they sensed uncertainty, they were likely to decide to take charge. Stewball began to prance restlessly. Stevie had to do something about that. She brought him up to a trot, and then, when they were on open and smooth land, she decided to let him lope. That would have the advantage of covering the distance faster and would let Stewball work out some knots.

At first Stewball seemed as glad as Stevie was to be going faster. Then something happened. A coyote howled. Two more joined it, and one of those was very close. No matter how well trained a horse was, he was still a creature of the wild, and in the wild a threatened horse had two choices: He could fight or he could flee. Most would flee. At night, unprotected by the presence of a herd, Stewball's innate senses took over his domesticated side. He felt the immediate threat of the presence of a predator. His instinct left him no choice. He took off.

Stevie was totally unprepared for it. Suddenly the horse who had been loping along pleasantly was racing. The three-beat gait turned to a four-beat gait, and at that it was so fast it was almost indistinguishable from a one-beat gait. Stewball was really covering ground.

He veered off the trail, frantically seeking safety. He leapt over a small cactus, turned sharply around a rock, and fled. Through all this Stevie held on, trying desperately to regain control of her horse. She lost a foothold in one of her stirrups and couldn't tighten up on the reins. With every step she came closer and closer to falling off. When Stewball took another turn to the right and shifted immediately to the left, further spooked by some unseen danger, that was it for Stevie. She flew up and out of the saddle and landed smack on her bottom. It hurt like crazy, but she was too angry to cry. All she could do was watch the retreating rear of her very frightened horse.

When the dust settled, she stood up, wiped her seat tentatively, decided it was going to be a good thing she wouldn't have to look at the bruise she was sure to have, and began walking. She didn't sing this time. She just grumbled.

"Here I am, in the middle of nowhere, walking when I should be riding, heading for Christine's house, so I can see if I can find somebody who will drive me back to the fair. All because I forgot to call earlier and because the phones weren't working right and there is a little child back at the high school who is going to be the happiest kid in town if and when I get back with the dollhouse, but I don't know if I can, except that just knowing some child is going to own that makes me want to keep on walking in spite of the fact that my stupid horse . . ."

She went on like that. It kept her focused on what

she was really doing, but it didn't change the fact that she wasn't exactly thrilled with the circumstances. It also kept her mind off the spooky things that had bothered her before—the owl and the branch and her own Halloween-y thoughts.

". . . and I don't know what I'll do if Mr. Lonetree isn't there, but somehow I'll find a way because, after all, my friends and I have traveled a couple thousand miles to be able to do this, so how could I possibly give up when I'm within about a half . . ."

A noise.

"Oh, come on, Stevie. The night is full of noises. Is this another echo scaring you?"

There it was again. She stopped.

It wasn't an echo, but when she listened to it, she wished it were. She wished it were an owl screeching or a witch or a vampire or any of a dozen imaginary things that had frightened her before, because this wasn't imaginary. This was real. This was dangerous. It was a rattlesnake.

Stevie had heard them before. She'd even seen them. She'd seen one kill. She froze, aware that the slightest movement could attract the snake's attention. She waited.

The sound came again. But where was it coming from?

There were several rocky places right around her as

well as a bush, any one of which could be hiding the viper.

Again, she heard it. Was it to the right? Or was it from straight ahead? Or was it that it came from the left, but the sound bounced off the rocks to the right? Nearby? Far? Would it strike? Would it hurt? Would it kill?

Terror took over. Stevie had never felt anything like it. She had nowhere to turn and no hope for escape. The terror filled her heart and her lungs. She gasped for breath, and when she got it, she screamed, long, loud, and hard. When she was done, she screamed some more, hearing only the echo of her own voice— and the rattle, constant, now drumming in her ears. Where? When?

Then there was another sound. It was the sound of hoofbeats. Stewball?

Stevie's eyes flicked upward. It wasn't Stewball. It was the stallion with the nick in his ear. There was a rider on his back, cloaked in white. A long and strong arm reached out to her. She reached up. In a smooth motion she was drawn up behind the rider and they flew across the desert, away from the snake, away from all danger.

Stevie clung to the rider with all her strength, not speaking a word. She couldn't have, anyway. She couldn't even utter a thank-you. She was shaking too hard. She could still hear the rattles. She could still hear the tones of her own screams echoing off the hills.

The stallion drew to a halt in front of the Lonetrees' house. Stevie dismounted, took a deep breath, and tried to think how she could thank John for being there just when she needed him the most. But the horse and rider turned and rode off, as quickly as they had come, without saying a word. Stevie shook her head and promised herself she would thank him the next time she saw him. For now, though, all she could do was look at that shiny white cloak he wore with the beautifully embroidered eagle on the back. John really did love practical jokes—he must have borrowed the cape Mrs. Lonetree had made for Christine so his outfit would be perfect for the part.

A night breeze cut across the land then. Stevie shivered and wrapped her arms around herself. That was when she remembered that *she* was wearing Christine's white cloak—and the eagle on Christine's cloak was painted, not embroidered with feathers. If the rider was John, this wasn't just a hoax, it was a very elaborate hoax. And if it wasn't John, just who—or what— was it?

**10**

"STEVIE? IS THAT YOU?"

The words gave Stevie a start. Then she realized it was Mr. Lonetree.

"Yes," she said, still confused by what had happened.

"I was looking for you. Your horse showed up here a few minutes ago, and then Christine called. She said something about the phones being broken for a while. Anyway, I'm glad you're safe. What happened?"

Now *there* was a question.

It took Stevie a while to pull all of the pieces together and to tell the story of her ride across the countryside without making herself sound like a fool or a fraidy cat. When Mr. Lonetree asked her how she'd gotten away from the rattlesnake, and assured her that she wasn't a fool or a fraidy cat to have been frightened by that snake, she found herself telling him about the silvery stallion Kate wanted to adopt and its connection to the story John had told the girls in the bunkhouse that night.

"Yes, the tale of White Eagle," Mr. Lonetree said. "I know it well. It's a story our people have told for generations. Nobody quite believes it's true, but everybody loves the tale."

"It's so romantic!" Stevie said. "I guess John was just trying to tell us a romantic eerie story for Halloween."

Mr. Lonetree looked confused. "Never would have thought of that story as eerie," he said.

"You might if you were thinking of owning the horse," Stevie told him. "We thought he made it up just to keep Kate from owning the stallion."

"Oh," said Mr. Lonetree. "I wouldn't have thought of it that way. See, to our people the traditional idea of ownership is very different from the way the Europeans who settled the land of America saw it. To us, all animals and land are something we have the honor to use for a while, but never own. Oh, sure, in America of the twentieth century, I have a deed for my property and a title to my car, but it's contrary to our tradition. I'm sure John Brightstar feels the same way. Even if one does 'own' a wild animal, it's not ownership in the sense you mean. I doubt he was trying to keep Kate from owning the stallion. I suspect he was rather saying that no matter what, she couldn't. Besides, Stevie, you and I are forgetting for a moment that it's just a story."

"Maybe," Stevie agreed reluctantly.

"Hey, we've got to get you back to the high school along with the dollhouse. Let's put your horse in the back of the van so you'll have transportation home— by the roadway, if you please."

"I promise," she said without hesitation.

THE MINUTE STEVIE walked into the party with the dollhouse, there was a hush. And then there was a rush. Everybody in the place wanted to make more guesses about the number of candies in the jar. She had a line of children following her before she could even get to the table. She wanted to tell her friends about what had happened out on the desert, but it would have to wait. Right now they couldn't take the twenty-five-cent tickets and hand out the guess slips fast enough. It was wonderful!

They even ended up agreeing to let the children put in guesses half an hour longer than they'd originally intended, just to make sure everybody who wanted to could enter the contest. Finally, when the last child had filled out the last slip, she took the jar of candies and the box of guesses out of the main room and went in search of a quiet place where she could sort all the entries and find the one or more that had the right number. The correct answer was known only to Phyllis Devine, who had written it on a piece of paper, put it in an envelope, and placed it at the bottom of the jar. Stevie thought that maybe she'd have to eat a lot of the candies in order to get to it, too.

The most quiet and private spot around was the horror house, which had been shut down. She entered, turned on some lights, and pulled up a chair to the table where the peeled grapes and cold pasta had been so terrifying to little visitors so recently. They didn't look particularly frightening in the light. Nor did they look appetizing. Stevie emptied the bowls in a nearby garbage can and went to work.

## 11

"HOLD THE LADDER steady now," John said from above.

"Don't worry," Lisa assured him. "I got plenty of practice at it when you were putting the crepe paper *up*. I don't think I've lost all my skills now that you're taking it down."

"Thanks," he said, dropping a large handful of crepe paper on the floor. Lisa scooped it up and put it in the garbage, all without letting go of the ladder.

Although other parts of the fair were continuing, the horror house was closed for the season, and the two of them had appointed themselves the committee to take it apart. It was a lot easier than putting it all together, and it seemed like a nice way to finish the day. At last it was relatively quiet, and there, in the small rooms they'd made for the horror house, it was even a little cozy—if you didn't mind crepe paper drifting down from above every once in a while.

"There, that's the last of that bunch," John said, climbing down. "I think there's some more in the next section, though."

"Not much," Lisa said. "Most of it got pulled down by the kids who were running to get away from me."

"You were great," he said. "I mean, all the kids I brought through were more scared when you were tickling them than at any other point—even more than when they slid into the Styrofoam."

"You weren't bad yourself—as a headless horseman, I mean. You scared a lot of the kids with that costume."

"Maybe, but I'm glad to be rid of those shoulder pads. I always wondered if I should be going out for football. Now I know for sure I couldn't possibly stand all that weight."

"Correct me if I'm wrong, but it seems to me that most football players only wear one set of shoulder pads at a time, right? And I also think they make their jerseys so that their heads stick out the top?"

John smiled at her joke. "I guess so, but I still think I'll stick to lacrosse. It's more my style, and you aren't as likely to get totally beaten up. Anyway, I didn't like scaring the kids too much. I know Halloween is supposed to be a little scary, but some of them were very frightened by me. I was glad to take the costume off for them, too."

"You're good with the kids," Lisa said. "Have you had experience? I mean, have you got younger brothers and sisters?"

Lisa was sorry the instant she'd asked the question. Of course he didn't have any younger brothers and sisters or they'd be at The Bar None with John and his dad. John seemed to be sensitive to any questions about his family. She wished she'd thought before she spoke.

"I did," he answered, surprising her.

"You did?" she couldn't help asking.

"I—" he sat down on the bottom step of the ladder. "I did, once," he said, completing his sentence.

Lisa wasn't sure if he regretted giving the information or if he really wanted to talk.

"You don't have to . . . ," she began.

"But I want to," he blurted suddenly. "Somehow I think you'll understand."

Would she? She didn't know. So far, she felt only confusion. She waited.

"I did have a sister. Her name was Gaylin. She was a wonderful child, always happy, always laughing. Then one day Gaylin was sick. She was very sick and there was no doctor nearby. My father had to drive my mother and Gaylin to the hospital. I came along, too. I sat in the front seat with Dad. Mother was in the back. Gaylin lay on the backseat next to her with her head on Mother's lap. She was so sick she was sweating with her fever. Dad knew it was bad, and he knew Gaylin's life depended on his ability to drive. He drove fast, as fast as he could, and still it didn't seem like it was fast enough. But it turned out to be too fast, because when a deer ran across the road, Dad tried to stop and swerved to avoid it. He missed the deer but ran the car right off the edge of the road and down a shallow ravine. He and I were okay. We'd had our seatbelts on. But Mother and Gaylin weren't so lucky."

Lisa gulped, understanding his pain.

"There was a police inquiry," John continued. "Some people said Dad had been drinking, but it wasn't true. There was a question, though, and there was talk. Plenty of it. Anybody could feel sorry for a man whose wife and daughter were killed in a car accident. Nobody would pity a man who'd killed them. It wasn't Dad's fault. Even the police concluded that. That didn't stop the rumors, though."

"Oh, John," Lisa began. "It must have been awful. . . ." It seemed like such a weak thing to say, but she meant it.

"It was," he said. "It still is, too, especially for Dad.

He doesn't drink, never did, but sometimes it seems like he might as well. He just withdraws, sleeps all the time. That's where he was the other night when you found me with the mare. He should have been there, but he wasn't. So I was just filling in."

Lisa reached for John's hand. She wanted to give him comfort, but she also wanted to be close to him. His hand was big and strong and warm. She squeezed it affectionately.

"You must miss them both," she said.

"I do. But in some ways I still have them, here in my heart, I mean. Every time I see a happy child, I feel I am with Gaylin again. And my mother? Well, I remember her through the stories she used to tell us. She was the great-granddaughter of a chief, and it was her family's responsibility to keep the hearth and carry the traditions to each succeeding generation."

"You mean like the story about the young lovers and the stallion? She told you that?"

"It was her favorite. She swore it was true, too. She lived all of her life believing that story—believing that no matter what else happened, there was always the stallion to help those who tried to do good things for our people. Sometimes I'm sure it was White Eagle who carried her and Gaylin out of the car . . ."

"How beautiful," Lisa said.

She became aware then that John was looking at her deeply. He glanced at their hands, now clasped warmly. He stood up and reached for her other hand. Lisa gave it to him.

"Lisa, I—"

"Shhh. You don't have to say anything."

He moved closer to her. She looked up at him, wondering, hoping, knowing . . .

"Got one!" Stevie shrieked from the other side of a temporary wall.

Lisa and John looked at one another in total surprise. They had had no idea she was there!

"Got what?" Lisa asked. She was trying very hard not to sound annoyed, but it wasn't easy. If she'd had her choice of when to be interrupted by her dear friend Stevie, it would have been almost any time but then!

"Oh, is that you, Lisa? Are you there? Are you alone?" Stevie asked.

Lisa and John shared a little giggle. "I'm here with John," Lisa said, brushing the layers of curtains aside and joining Stevie in what they'd come to think of as the grape-and-spaghetti room. John followed her.

"I got a winner," Stevie told them proudly. "Look, here it is. One child got the *exact* number of candy corns that Phyllis wrote on her piece of paper. Now all I have to do is search and see if anybody else has it. I was afraid I was going to have to sort through a thousand entries to find the one that's the closest. Give me a hand, will you? You, too, John?"

"You and Lisa can do that," John said. "I think I'll finish removing the black crepe paper and see what else needs to be tidied. See you later, okay?"

"Sure," Stevie said. Then she thought for a second. This seemed like the perfect opportunity to test and see if the mysterious rider had been John. If he admitted it, that would confirm it. If he denied it, well, it almost certainly still was John. After all, who else could it be? A ghost? No way! "Thanks for helping me earlier," she said finally.

Lisa didn't know what Stevie was talking about, but there was a mischievous twinkle in Stevie's eye, and Lisa found herself a little bit jealous.

"How's that?" John asked. Apparently he didn't know what she was talking about, either. That made Lisa feel somewhat better.

"Out there?" Stevie said.

"Where?"

"In the desert? When you saved my life?"

"I don't know what you're talking about," John said.

"You don't have to keep it up anymore," Stevie said. "I mean, after all, you did deliver me safely to the Lonetrees' house."

"I did?"

"Nice try, but thanks anyway. No matter what you say, I still say thank you. You didn't give me a chance before, so now I'm saying it and I mean it."

John shrugged. "I guess you're welcome then," he said. "But I don't know why."

He slipped away. Lisa could hear him moving the ladder. She wanted to go hold it for him. She wanted to be with him, to bring back that moment of quiet and intimacy that was unlike any moment she'd ever known before in her life.

"Here, you go through this stack," Stevie said, handing her a huge pile of entry slips.

"What was that all about?" Lisa asked when she was sure John was out of their hearing.

"It was just another one of John's practical jokes," Stevie said. "Except this one was no joke and it was very practical. I'll tell you later, okay? Right now, we have to concentrate on these entry slips. Besides, I want to tell the whole story to everyone at once." Stevie looked at the entry slip on the top of her stack and scowled. "Is that 7,561 or 7,567?" she asked.

"Doesn't matter. It's not the right answer," Lisa said quickly. She wanted to pump Stevie for more information on her mysterious conversation with John, but she knew there was no point. If Stevie had decided to keep a secret—for now, anyway—wild horses, even silvery stallions, couldn't drag it out of her.

Lisa concentrated on the stack of slips in front of her.

## 12

STEVIE FELT WONDERFUL. The gigantic pile of entry slips in front of her meant she and Lisa were going to have to do a lot of work looking through them, but it also meant they made a ton of money. Mrs. Lonetree's dollhouse was perfect!

A few other things had her feeling good as well. For one thing, she had a wonderful adventure to share with her friends! For another, she was alive. She still hadn't recovered from her fright out on the trail with the rattlesnake, but she *was* alive, and she was safe. Moreover, she'd had a chance to thank John—even though he denied it, of course.

"John is one funny guy," Stevie said to Lisa.

"Yes," Lisa agreed. Stevie could have sworn her

friend sighed as she said it. She couldn't imagine why.

"How did it go in the horror house?" Stevie asked.

"What?" Lisa asked. She seemed embarrassed. Again, Stevie couldn't figure out Lisa's reaction.

"Horror house," Stevie repeated. "I heard kids screaming all afternoon. I assume that means they were having fun."

"Oh, yes, of course," Lisa said. "The kids had a fabulous time. Everything you planned worked beautifully. You are a genius, you know. About most things."

"Yes, I know," Stevie said modestly, though it crossed her mind briefly to wonder what things Lisa thought she *wasn't* a genius about. It wasn't too hard to figure out. Lisa was a straight-A student. Stevie wasn't. Stevie decided that was what Lisa meant.

They worked together in silence, now quickly sifting through the entries. They had to pause a few times because they had trouble with handwriting or wanted to share a particularly interesting entry.

"Get this," Stevie said, reading from a small slip of paper. "It says 'Even if this isn't right, please, please, please choose me because I really love the dollhouse.'"

"Is it the right number?" Lisa asked.

"Nope, and too bad," Stevie said. "I remember the child who filled it out. She's dressed as Darth Vader. She scared me, I'll tell you!"

Eventually they finished examining the last of the entries and were more than a little relieved to find that there was only one correct answer. They had no idea what they would have done if there had been more than one winner. Stevie had suggested the possibility that she might eat a candy or two until they got to another number that there was only one entry for. Fortunately, she didn't have to.

The minute Stevie and Lisa entered the main room of the basement, there was a hush. Every child there knew Stevie was in charge and what she had just been up to.

"We have a winner!" Stevie declared.

The kids gathered around.

"We certainly do," said Phyllis Devine, momentarily taking the floor from Stevie. "And the winner is the after-school program. While Stevie has been counting candies, I've been counting cash. Today's fair has earned over two thousand dollars!" Stevie could hardly believe it. She'd thought they would be lucky to make five hundred dollars.

"Now, Stevie, tell us who the winner is."

Stevie took the winning slip from Lisa. "The actual number of candies in the jar was two thousand five!" There was a gasp. Stevie had completely forgotten, but she knew who the winner was. She'd watched the

little panda fill out all six slips. Two thousand five was
her very last twenty-five cents!

"It's *me*!" declared the panda, dashing forward. "I
won! I won!"

Stevie couldn't help grinning. Neither could anybody else who witnessed the joy.

"You absolutely did!" Stevie said, giving the little
girl a hug and leading her to where her dollhouse was
stored. The two of them were followed by a lot of curious and excited kids. By the time Stevie actually
turned over the dollhouse to the panda, the girl was
too busy making playdates with friends who wanted
a chance at her newest toy to pay any attention to
Stevie. It was all Stevie could do to get out of the mob.
Their happiness made her feel very good. This was
definitely for a good cause—more than one, in fact.

Stevie had been looking at entry slips for so long
that she hadn't had a chance to look at the mural for a
long time. She was astonished to see how much work
had been done on it, and now that she wasn't selling
tickets or counting them, she took a good long time to
check it out.

Phyllis Devine was there, too.

"It's wonderful!" Stevie said, looking at the glorious
collection of drawings. She found what she thought
was a panda, next to a lopsided sugarplum fairy, not
far from what looked like Superman trying to trap a

navel orange—or maybe it was a pumpkin. She found a balloon hovering over three witches and a ghost. Next to them were none other than three blind mice and a farmer's wife. She thought she sensed the fine hand of Kate Devine there. She was pretty good with a paintbrush. She also saw Christine in her gleaming white outfit, including the cape. The cape made Stevie remember her ride and the one mysterious aspect of it. Where had John gotten the cape he'd worn?

And where was John in the mural? She was sure he would have wanted to leave his mark, but she searched every inch of the mural and couldn't find the headless horseman. Then, in a corner, up high in the sky, she found his mark. It wasn't the headless horseman at all. It was the silvery stallion, sleek and beautiful, with a nick in his ear. He had no rider in the picture. There was no cape, no young lovers—just the horse, proud, wild, and free.

Although Stevie thought John was a pretty odd young man, she had to admit that he sure did know how to ride a horse, and he sure knew how to draw one!

## 13

"THAT'S THE LAST bag of garbage," Carole announced proudly, putting the black plastic bag outside the back of the high school.

"Then that's the last bit of cleanup we have to do," Stevie said. The deal had been that if they ran the fair, disassembled the horror house, and took out the garbage, other volunteers would do all the rest of the cleanup. They were done. What they had come to the West to accomplish was complete. Finished. Successful.

"What do we do now?" Lisa asked, aware that she felt a little let down.

"Well, that's obvious, isn't it?" Stevie asked. "It's

Halloween night, we're in costumes, we go trick or treating!"

Only Stevie would think of collecting candy after an exhausting day of running the Halloween Fair. And that was just one of the reasons her friends loved her.

"So what are we waiting for?" Christine asked.

"Can John come with us?" Lisa asked. The girls looked at her curiously. "He worked very hard at the fair. He ought to have some fun, too," she said quickly.

Carole had the feeling there was more to it than that, but before she could ask, Kate answered the question. "I invited him, but he said he had to get back to the ranch. He wanted to check on the filly. I don't know why his father can't do that—"

Lisa knew. She almost spoke up, but that wouldn't have been fair to John. He'd told her the story of his sister's and his mother's death and the effect it had on his father when they were alone. He surely wouldn't want her to share the information with her friends.

"He just loves the filly," she said. "She's awfully cute, you know."

Stevie clicked her tongue to get Stewball moving, and then when everybody else was at a comfortable walk, she said, "I'm sure he does love the filly, but I wouldn't count on his going back to The Bar None.

He's probably waiting for us somewhere on the stallion in his white costume, ready to give us another show."

"What do you mean 'another show'?" Lisa asked.

"Well, you know how he followed us when we went to Christine's?" Kate said.

"It was pretty dark then," Lisa reminded her friends. "We don't know for sure that that was John on the stallion. We don't even know for sure that there was anybody on the stallion. There just *seemed* to be a rider on the horse's back."

"Let's try this house first," Kate said, interrupting the conversation. "The woman has worked for Mom at the ranch. They have lots of kids, and look at the pumpkin on their porch. I bet the candy's great!"

The girls rode up to the house and called "Trick or treat!" from their saddles.

The door soon opened. The three blind mice, the farmer's wife, and White Eagle all accepted the offer of homemade caramel apples—and moist paper towels so they could clean their hands right after they finished eating!

"You're the perfectly prepared Halloween host!" Kate said as thanks.

"Seems the least we can do for the group that made it possible to have an after-school program on the reservation. So thank *you* all. And have a good ride!"

The family waved a cheery good-bye and then closed the door.

"How did they know?" Stevie asked.

"It's a small town," Kate said. "Everybody knows everything."

"Everything?"

"Everything," Christine agreed.

The next house seemed to confirm the idea. The little girl who answered the door took one look at them and shrieked to her mother—"Mommy! It's the mouse who taught me how to ride a pony!"

Carole laughed. She barely recognized the child out of costume, but obviously the child remembered her, and she had the nice warm feeling that she'd started this little girl on a long and happy journey as a devoted horseback rider.

Her friends were happy about that, too, because the net result was measurable in their candy bags. The little girl's mother was *very* generous.

The house after that was the home of the panda who had won the dollhouse. It seemed that that child's parents couldn't say enough about how wonderful the party had been and how fabulous the dollhouse was. They knew the Lonetrees and gave Christine messages for her mother about what a great thing she'd done.

"Just wait until they see what it's like to have everybody in the class come over every day after school!" Stevie joked as they rode away. "It's going to be like a feeding frenzy."

"Like we're going to have with all these goodies later on?" Kate asked, patting her candy bag.

"Exactly the same," Stevie said. She was known for her sweet tooth. She was even looking forward to the inevitable stomachache.

Carole leaned forward and patted Berry on the neck. Then she took a moment to look around at her friends, decked out in Halloween costumes and riding horseback.

"You know, I've been trick or treating in a lot of different places. It's always been fun, but it's never been like this. Do you have any idea what we look like, walking our horses around Two Mile Creek, dressed up the way we are?"

"Pretty silly, I'm sure, but it seems to be working, doesn't it?" Kate answered. "Actually, I've had some pretty unusual Halloweens. I remember one time I went as a robot. I couldn't walk because I was wearing all these big cardboard boxes. That was funny."

"Once I was a pirate," Stevie recalled. "I decided I should have a wooden leg, so I folded one leg up in my jeans."

"That must have been scary!" Lisa said.

"Sure was. My leg got so numb I couldn't walk for an

hour after I got home. The worst part was that my candy bag was in the other room and my brothers wouldn't bring it to me!"

The image of Stevie separated from her goodies by a numb leg got all five girls laughing.

"Well, all I can say is that there's never been another Halloween like this for me," Carole concluded. "And since it's highly unlikely that another Halloween will ever be this good, I think this will be my last year trick or treating. What a way to go out!"

"Definitely in glory," Stevie agreed. "And speaking of fabulous Halloweens, I haven't even had a chance yet to tell you all what happened to me when I was on the way to get the dollhouse at Christine's."

"Yeah, tell us!" Christine said. "Dad told me your horse showed up before you did. I forgot to ask what that was all about!"

"Well, settle back in the saddle, take a bite out of your caramel apple, and listen to my tale, because every word of it is true," Stevie said. Then she told them what happened—down to the tiniest, scariest detail.

"At first I was afraid," she began. She didn't mention that she was also scared at the middle and the end. For most of the adventure she'd been alone, and nobody was going to contradict her.

As her tale progressed, she elaborated elegantly

about the owl she'd seen. In the retelling his feathered wings had brushed her cheeks!

"Oooh!" Lisa said, frightened by the thought.

Then the branch that grabbed her hair had seemed to dig in and pull relentlessly. It wasn't exactly true, but it was more or less what Stevie had *thought* was happening at the time. Finally, when she got to the part about the coyote howling, Stewball bolting, and the rattlesnake threatening, she found that she didn't have to embellish at all. The entire story was simply terrifying.

"You mean you could hear him, but you had no idea where he was?" Christine asked.

"That's right. I was petrified. I did the only possible rational thing."

"You froze," Kate said, knowing that was the right thing to do.

"Well, that, but I also did something else. I screamed my head off."

"You did?" Christine said, horrified. That seemed like a very bad idea to her.

"Yes, and it's a good thing I did. Because John was there on the stallion. I guess he knew I'd gone out, and he was just waiting to make a mysterious appearance. But when I screamed, he came to my rescue."

She told them then how he'd swept by, lifted her off her feet onto the horse behind him, and had ridden her to the Lonetrees', dropping her off without a word.

"I was a little annoyed that he was still doing his phony Indian routine to try to convince us that the story was real, but I certainly wasn't annoyed that he was there to help me when I needed him the most."

"Wow," Kate said. "I'm impressed."

"How can you thank him!" Carole said.

"What a coincidence!" Kate said.

"No way," said Lisa.

"Huh?"

"No way," Lisa repeated.

"What do you mean 'no way'?" Stevie asked. "I'm here. I'm alive. I definitely got saved. It happened."

"Oh, I'm sure it happened," said Lisa. "Just the way you said. Except for one thing. It wasn't John."

"Of course it was," Stevie said. "Who else could it be? I mean, at first I even thought he was wearing Christine's cloak until I realized that *I* was wearing it. I don't know where he got his costume or when he changed, but he was definitely there."

"It's not possible," said Lisa. "I know where John Brightstar was all afternoon because he never left the horror house."

"Are you sure?" Stevie asked.

Lisa thought before she answered. She didn't want to tell her friends what she was feeling about John, and letting them know how carefully she had watched would reveal more than she wanted. Still, she was sure, and she could tell them that.

"I'm sure," she said. "Somebody saved Stevie out here this evening, but it wasn't John. I'm sure of that."

"Then who was it?" Stevie asked.

The question hung in the air. Five girls were wondering the same thing. Five girls considered the fact that it was Halloween, a night when strange things were supposed to happen.

# 14

"OKAY, PASS THE popcorn and I'll tell," Lisa said.

"Keep the popcorn from her and she'll tell faster," Stevie teased.

Carole wasn't sure what to do. The three of them were in her bedroom having their first Saddle Club meeting since returning from The Bar None a week ago, and Lisa seemed to be on the verge of telling her friends some very interesting news about a certain wrangler's son from the dude ranch.

"You mean you and John Brightstar . . . ?" Stevie asked.

Lisa blushed.

"That's enough of an answer for me," Carole said.

She handed the bowl to Lisa, who took a handful and then gave the bowl to Stevie.

"He's really nice," Lisa said.

"We know that," Stevie said. "Although he appears to me to be a bit mysterious. But the question is just *how* nice?"

"Really nice," Lisa confirmed.

"How did you get to be so friendly?" Carole asked. She just wanted to know how these things happened.

"I held the ladder for him an awful lot, as you'll recall," Lisa said.

"Is that what you were doing when I got you to help me look at the entry slips?" Stevie asked.

Lisa remembered the moment. How could she forget? "Yes, that's what we were doing. At first I was just holding the ladder, then I was, well, uh, kind of holding his hand."

"You were?"

"Yeah," Lisa said. "Until one of my best friends interrupted me."

It was Stevie's turn to blush. "I'm sorry," she said. "I had no idea."

"I didn't think you did," Lisa said. "Otherwise I would have wrung your neck—just the same as you would do to me."

"You bet I would," Stevie agreed. "Anyway, did you get to see him again before we left?"

"Yes," Lisa said. "I saw him in the barn on Sunday morning—you know, just to say good-bye. It was kind of nice."

Her friends knew what she meant. They didn't have to ask, and they were very happy for her.

There was a knock at the door. Colonel Hanson stuck his head in. "Letter for you today, honey," he said, handing an envelope to Carole. Carole took it and looked at it excitedly. "Oh, it's from Kate, and I bet she's writing to tell us what happened at the horse adoption!"

Carole tore open the envelope and began reading out loud.

*"You're hearing from the proud adoptive parent of a beautiful wild horse. She's a mare—mostly quarter horse, I think, and she's got a foal, too! They're both sorrel. I've named the mare Moon Glow. She's so beautiful I can't wait to show her to you girls. You've got to come back and meet her. Walter says we should start gentling her—that means getting her used to a halter and a lead rope—within a week or so. After that, we begin the real training. She's got wonderful lines. I know she's going to be a fine riding horse for me someday, and her foal is a beauty, too."*

"But what about the stallion?" Lisa asked. "What does she say about that?"

Carole continued reading.

> "I suppose you want to know about the stallion and, frankly, so do I. I can tell you what happened, but I certainly can't explain it.
>
> Dad and I went to the adoption, looking for the stallion. We'd even spoken to the man in charge of it to warn him that was the horse we wanted. He said he didn't know the horse we meant, but since we'd had our application in for so long, we should have a good selection, as long as we got there early.
>
> It was the stallion's herd all right. I recognized some of the mares. You would have, too. But there was no sign of the stallion. There was a stallion with the herd, but he wasn't silvery, and he didn't have a nick in his ear. In fact, he was a kind of ugly skewbald pinto.
>
> Dad and I asked all the Bureau of Land Management people about the silvery stallion with the nick in his ear. Every single one of them said they'd never seen such a horse with this herd. Never seen a horse like that around here. So, what do you think?"

"Oh, my," Lisa said, almost involuntarily. She could still see the stallion. She knew he existed. Didn't he?

"I don't understand," said Carole. "We actually *saw* that horse—more than once."

"There has to be an explanation," Stevie agreed. Then she turned to Lisa. "Look, you're the logical one here. What do you think is going on?"

"Maybe that skewbald just looks silvery white in the moonlight," Carole said. "We never did see him up close or in good light, you know."

"Maybe," Stevie said. "But I still think John's behind this."

"John was with me," Lisa reminded her friend.

"Then his father! It must have been Walter. It was just a big hoax."

"Maybe," Lisa said. In her heart, though, that wasn't what she thought. In her heart, she could see the spirit of White Eagle rising from the flames of the fire, joining the spirit of Moon Glow on the back of the white horse who had brought them together and who carried them to the skies to unite them for eternity. She could also imagine John as a young boy, hearing his mother tell him the tale, and loving the image of the free horse roaming the desert. "And maybe not," she said. "But you know, there's one thing that seems right, and that is that as much as I would have liked Kate to have the stallion, if she's not going to be the one to own him, nobody is. Somewhere out there—maybe on the plains or the desert, maybe even in our imaginations—the silvery stallion is roaming free and wild. He is there to help those who do good for the Native American people. That's the way it ought to be, you know."

At first Carole and Stevie didn't answer her. They were lost in their own thoughts—visions of the silvery stallion with the nick in his ear.

"Maybe," Stevie said, finally.

"Yeah," Carole agreed. "Maybe."

# ABOUT THE AUTHOR

BONNIE BRYANT is the author of more than fifty books for young readers, including novelizations of movie hits such as *Teenage Mutant Ninja Turtles* and *Honey, I Shrunk the Kids*, written under her married name, B. B. Hiller.

Ms. Bryant began writing The Saddle Club in 1986. Although she had done some riding before that, she intensified her studies then and found herself learning right along with her characters Stevie, Carole, and Lisa. She claims that they are all much better riders than she is.

Ms. Bryant was born and raised in New York City. She lives in Greenwich Village with her two sons.